MONSTERS
and other
SCARY SHIT

(a monster anthology about monsters)

**Edited by
Russell Nohelty**

**Written and drawn by
various awesome people, places,
things, and ideas**

**Cover by
Aaron Alexovich**

Published by Wannabe Press
Hardcover ISBN: 978-1-942350-32-3
Paperback ISBN: 978-1-942350-30-9

main credits and signing pages

Go Fish
Erik Lervold and Russell Nohelty

Millennials and Dragons
Nicolas Touris

The Party
Katrina Kunstmann

Ghoul
Alexander and Stan Yak

Download: Possession
Juan Carlos Ramos

Last Rites
John Holland and Jonathan Fisher

A Screen to Kill For
Greg Smith, Michael Tanner, and Meescha Dare

Fear Monster
Christie Shinn

B is for Beer
Scott Bachmann and Nate Lovett

Butterfly
Arthur Bellfield and Blair Rossi

Vengeance
Dennis Greenhill

Fear
Bradley Sheridan

Undeaducation
Joe Ranoia and Cassidy Phillips

Boogeyman
Christian Douglas and Ivan Sarnago

The Legend of the White Lady
David Lucarelli and Henry Ponciano

Frozen Scream
Walter Ostlie

Nightwalker
Mary Bellamy

The Deal
Zac Skellington and Daniel Sharner

One Last Tear
Nicholas Doan and Daniele Serra

Online Predator
Erika Lipkes and Steve Waldinger

Claxton and Claxton
CW Cooke and Kurt Belcher

The Promise
Felix Yin and Alex Bodnar

Emerik
Michael Norwitz and Phillip Johnson

Do My Bidding
Bobby Timony

Seven Tears
Rob Hebert

The Mirror
Greg Smith and Meescha Dare

Calladseelee
Jack Holder and Saint Yak

Belly of the Beast
Josh Wagner and Freedom Drudge

Terror, Thy Name is Poo
Alex and Luis Bermudez

Esmerelda's Tree
Angela Fullard

MONSTER!
GO FISH
WRITER: RUSSELL NOHELTY
ART: ERIK LERVOLD
COLORS: MICHAEL K
ASSISTANT: ARI MULCH

CHARGE!
DO YOU HAVE ANY FIVES?
GO FISH.

WHAT DO YOU THINK YOU ARE DOING?
STAB!

HAVING AT THEE, MONSTER!

CAN'T I GET ONE MOMENT OF PEACE?

DO YOU HAVE ANY TENS?
GO FISH.
Poik!

DO YOU LIKE THE PERSON YOU ARE?
OF COURSE. I AM A KNIGHT SWORN TO PROTECT THE REALM FROM MONSTERS LIKE YOU!

THAT HURTS MY FEELINGS, YOU KNOW THAT?
OH. WELL NO. I HADN'T THOUGHT OF THAT. YOU HAVE FEELINGS?

OF COURSE I HAVE FEELINGS.
OH, I JUST ASSUMED WITH ALL THE BONES.

I HAVE A RIGHT TO DEFEND MYSELF IN MY OWN HOUSE, DON'T I?
IT'S YOUR TURN.
I SUPPOSE SO.

SORRY PRINCESS. DO YOU HAVE ANY THREES?
THE PRINCESS. THAT'S RIGHT YOU KIDNAPPED THE PRINCESS!
GODDAMN IT!

WHO KIDNAPPED ME?
THIS OAF. HE'S HELD YOU AGAINST YOUR WILL AS A PRISONER.

HAH HAH HAH HAH HAH HAH HAH
HAH HAH HAH HAH HAH HAH

WHO TOLD YOU THAT?
WHY THE KING, OF COURSE. HE PRONOUNCED IT A FORTNIGHT HENCE.
OF COURSE HE DID. HE HATES MY FRIENDS.

FRIEND? YOU ARE FRIENDS WITH THIS MONSTER?
MY NAME IS TOM, YOU KNOW. I DON'T CALL YOU KNIGHT.
THE KING IS QUITE ADAMANT YOU COME HOME.

WELL HE CAN SUCK NOODLES.
IT'S STILL YOUR TURN.
DO YOU HAVE ANY NINES?
GO FISH.

THIS IS A VERY SERIOUS CHARGE. I'M TO BRING YOU IN WITH HIS HEAD.
WITH MY HEAD? THAT'S NOT VERY NICE. WHAT HAVE I EVER DONE TO YOU?

YOU STOLE THE PRINCESS.
EVEN IF THAT'S TRUE, WHICH IT ISN'T, WHAT DOES THAT HAVE TO DO WITH YOU?

WELL, SHE IS THE LADY OF THE LAND. IF YOU DISRESPECT HER, YOU DISRESPECT THE COUNTRY.
SO WHAT? THE COUNTRY IS SHIT.

YOU NEED A MORE HOLISTIC VIEW OF THE WORLD. LIFE EXTENDS BEYOND THE KINGDOM.
YOU DON'T TELL ME WHAT TO DO! MONSTERS ARE NOT WORTHY OF MY EARS. MONSTERS ARE MEANT TO BE HUNTED!

AND THERE WE HAVE IT. YOU'RE A RACIST.
AM NOT! I JUST THINK I'M BETTER THAN YOU, THAT'S ALL.
YOU NEED TO GROW UP. IF YOUR VIEW OF THE WORLD LIGHTENS UP, I WOULD LOVE TO HAVE YOU FOR TEA.
SLAM!

I WILL NEVER STOP! I WILL COME BACK WITH A HUNDRED MEN!
A THOUSAND!

A MILLION!
COME OUT AND FACE ME!

SLAM!

WHY CAN'T THEY JUST LEAVE WELL ENOUGH ALONE?
THEY'RE IDIOTS. WHY DO YOU THINK I KEEP RUNNING AWAY?

WHAT I DON'T GET IS WHY YOU EVER GO BACK.
TO SHOWER. WHOSE TURN IS IT?
YOURS.

DO YOU HAVE ANY KINGS?
GO FISH.

THE PARTY
WRITTEN AND ILLUSTRATED BY KATRINA KUNSTMANN
ELLENA?
YES?
REMIND ME AGAIN WHY I'M COMING ALONG TO THIS?
BECAUSE, THEO, IT WILL BE FUN.
WE WILL HAVE FUN.
FFFS
I VERY MUCH DOUBT THAT.

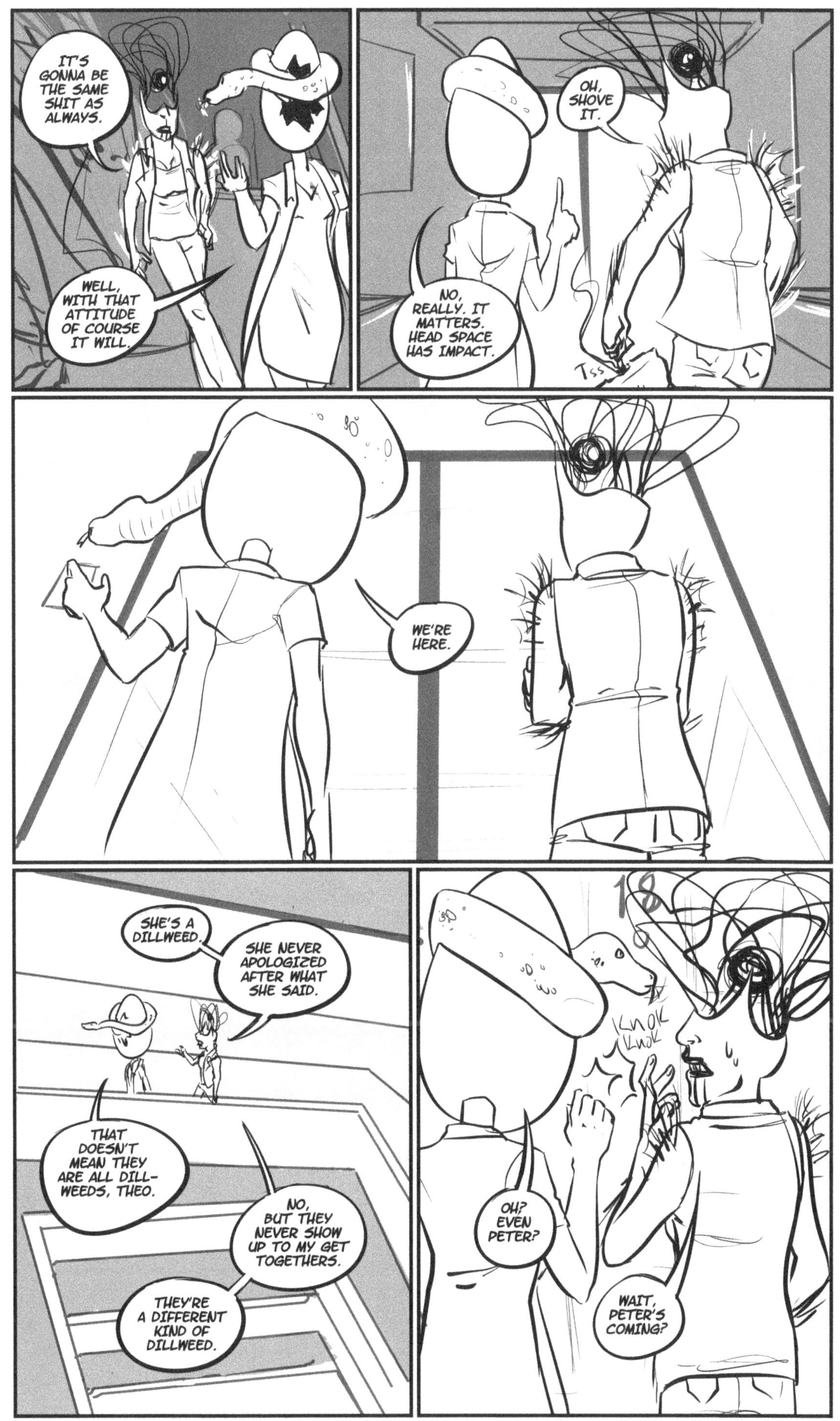

IT'S GONNA BE THE SAME SHIT AS ALWAYS.
WELL, WITH THAT ATTITUDE OF COURSE IT WILL.
OH, SHOVE IT.
NO, REALLY. IT MATTERS. HEAD SPACE HAS IMPACT.
Tss
WE'RE HERE.
SHE'S A DILLWEED.
SHE NEVER APOLOGIZED AFTER WHAT SHE SAID.
THAT DOESN'T MEAN THEY ARE ALL DILL-WEEDS, THEO.
NO, BUT THEY NEVER SHOW UP TO MY GET TOGETHERS.
THEY'RE A DIFFERENT KIND OF DILLWEED.
OH? EVEN PETER?
WAIT, PETER'S COMING?
KNOK KNOK
18

HEY GUYS!
THALO!
ELLENA, HOW ARE YOU?
HI, THEO!
HEY, LAURA!
. . .
!!
Ha Ha Ha
PETER.

Zubr
I-7 EN
GIN

JoM

SWIGGITY SWOOTY
GONNA GET
DAT BOOTY

HEY, PETER!

HEY, THEO!
YO!

WELL, THIS IS OK AT LEAST.
27
I CAN ENJOY MYSELF JUST A LITTLE BIT.
I GET TO TALK TO HIM.

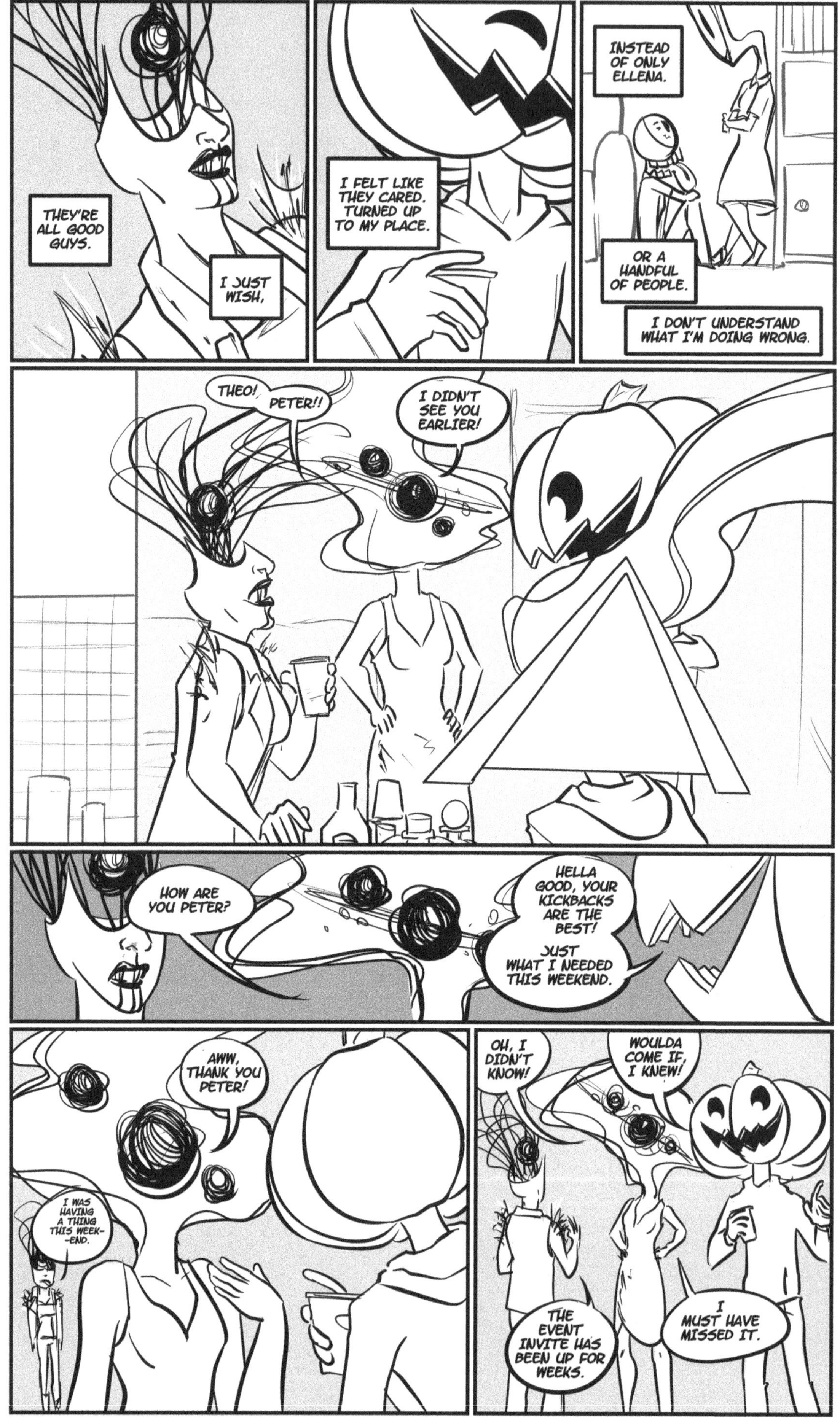

THEY'RE ALL GOOD GUYS.
I JUST WISH,
I FELT LIKE THEY CARED. TURNED UP TO MY PLACE.
INSTEAD OF ONLY ELLENA.
OR A HANDFUL OF PEOPLE.
I DON'T UNDERSTAND WHAT I'M DOING WRONG.
THEO!
PETER!!
I DIDN'T SEE YOU EARLIER!
HOW ARE YOU PETER?
HELLA GOOD, YOUR KICKBACKS ARE THE BEST!
JUST WHAT I NEEDED THIS WEEKEND.
AWW, THANK YOU PETER!
I WAS HAVING A THING THIS WEEK—END.
OH, I DIDN'T KNOW!
WOULDA COME IF, I KNEW!
THE EVENT INVITE HAS BEEN UP FOR WEEKS.
I MUST HAVE MISSED IT.

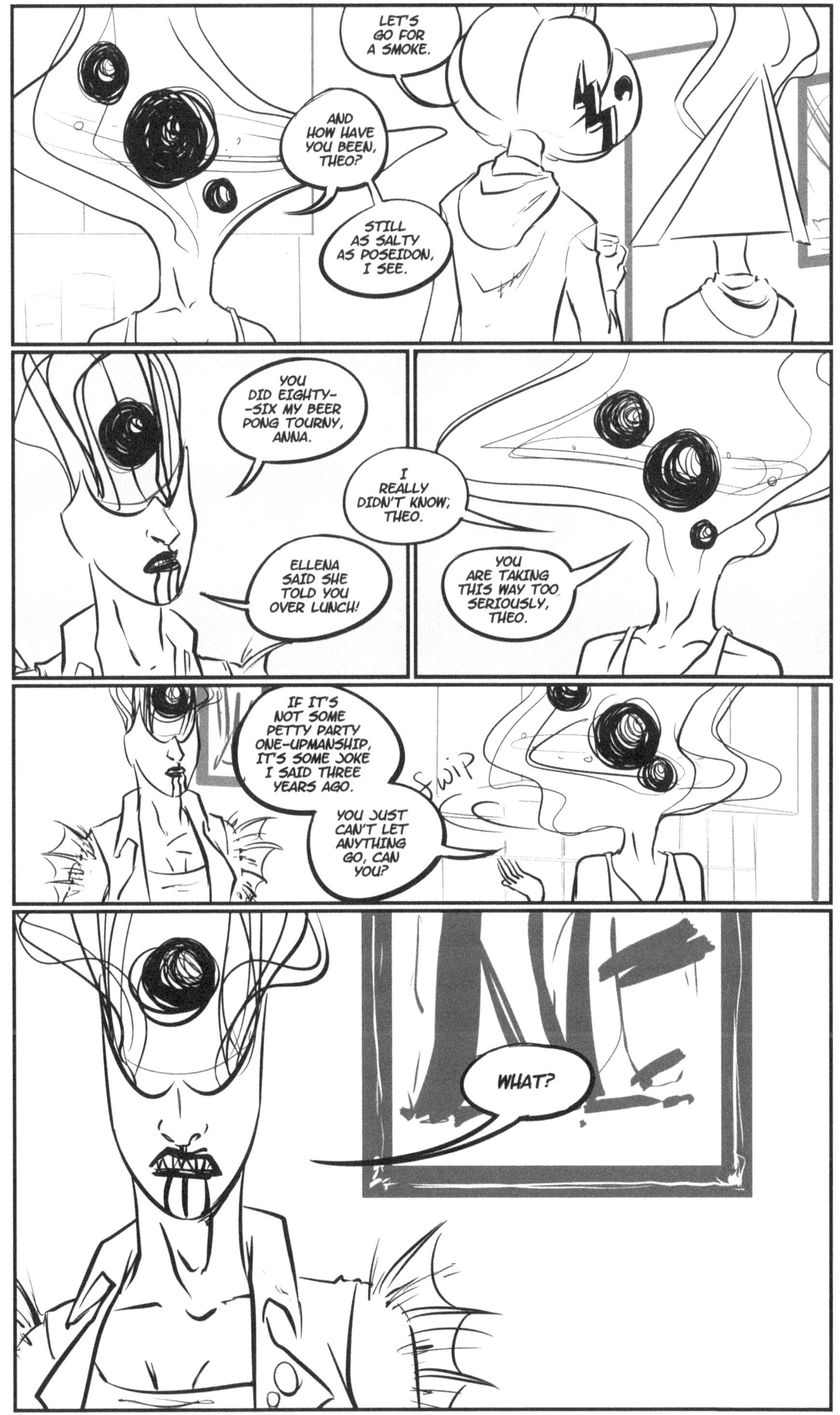

LET'S GO FOR A SMOKE.
AND HOW HAVE YOU BEEN, THEO?
STILL AS SALTY AS POSEIDON, I SEE.
YOU DID EIGHTY--SIX MY BEER PONG TOURNY, ANNA.
I REALLY DIDN'T KNOW, THEO.
ELLENA SAID SHE TOLD YOU OVER LUNCH!
YOU ARE TAKING THIS WAY TOO SERIOUSLY, THEO.
IF IT'S NOT SOME PETTY PARTY ONE-UPMANSHIP, IT'S SOME JOKE I SAID THREE YEARS AGO.
YOU JUST CAN'T LET ANYTHING GO, CAN YOU?
FWIP
WHAT?

OH PLEASE, YOU KNOW EXACTLY WHAT I'M TALKING ABOUT.
EVER SINCE THAT NIGHT AT THE BAR YOU'VE HELD EVERYTHING I'VE EVER DONE AGAINST ME, DOWN TO THE LAST QUARK.
AND THE WORST PART IS YOU KNOW I'M RIGHT ABOUT ALL OF IT
turn
YOU'RE BEING OVER-SENSITIVE. YOU ALWAYS ARE.
IT'S JUST A PARTY, IF EVERYONE IS ENJOYING THEM-SELVES, WHO CARES WHO'S HOSTING?
AND WRITING FIFTY-THOUSAND WORDS ISN'T THAT BIG OF A DEAL.
TRY BEING A LIT MAJOR.
SMAK

WELL I NEVER.
• • •
WELL, BE SEEING YOU, THEO.
NOOOOOOO....
HEEEYYY...
....BUDDY.
HIC
SNF
AW, BUDDY.
COME ON, THEODORA, LET'S GO TO THE ROOF.
OKAY?
YEAH, SURE. WHY NOT.

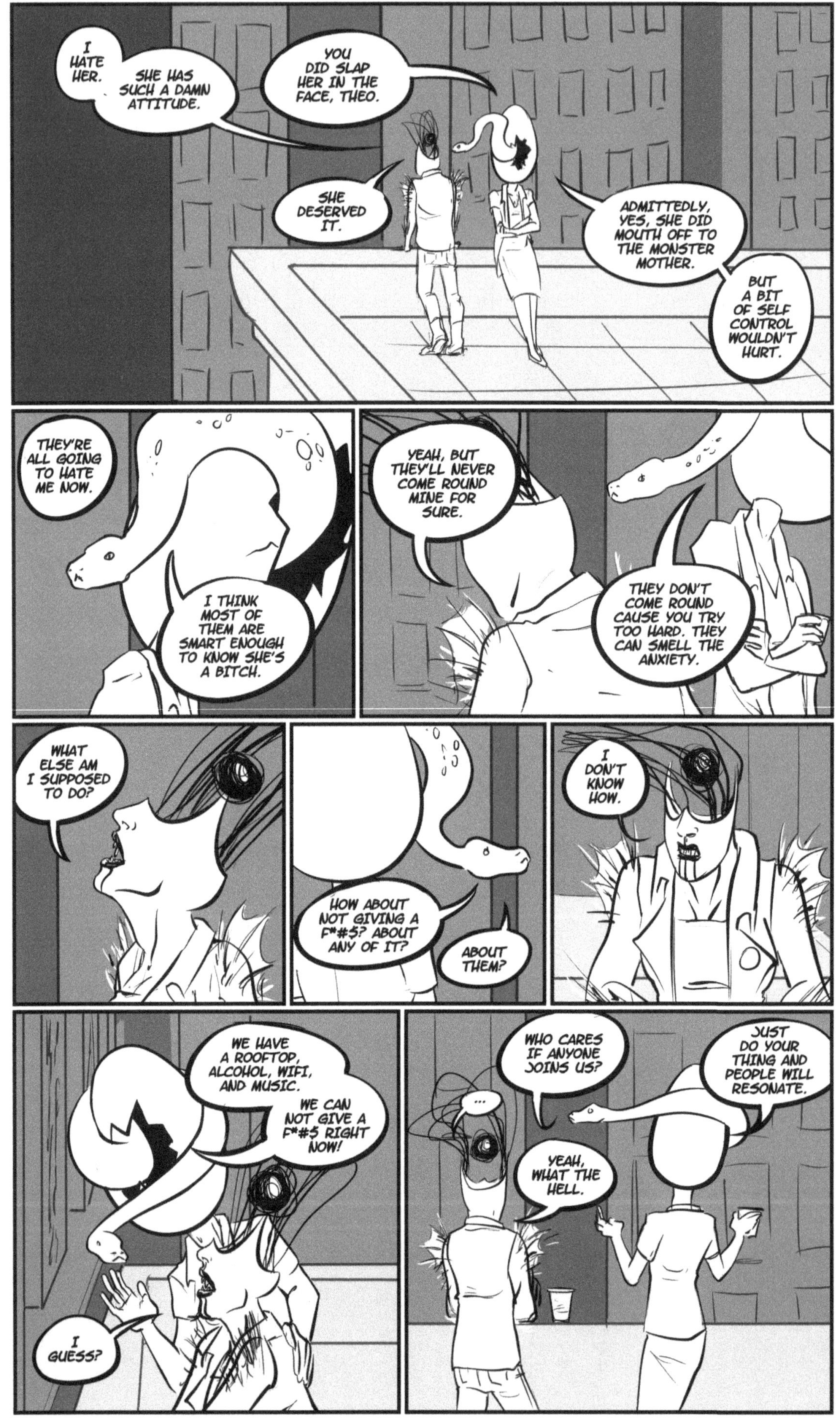

I HATE HER.
SHE HAS SUCH A DAMN ATTITUDE.
YOU DID SLAP HER IN THE FACE, THEO.
SHE DESERVED IT.
ADMITTEDLY, YES, SHE DID MOUTH OFF TO THE MONSTER MOTHER.
BUT A BIT OF SELF CONTROL WOULDN'T HURT.
THEY'RE ALL GOING TO HATE ME NOW.
I THINK MOST OF THEM ARE SMART ENOUGH TO KNOW SHE'S A BITCH.
YEAH, BUT THEY'LL NEVER COME ROUND MINE FOR SURE.
THEY DON'T COME ROUND CAUSE YOU TRY TOO HARD. THEY CAN SMELL THE ANXIETY.
WHAT ELSE AM I SUPPOSED TO DO?
HOW ABOUT NOT GIVING A F*#5? ABOUT ANY OF IT?
ABOUT THEM?
I DON'T KNOW HOW.
WE HAVE A ROOFTOP, ALCOHOL, WIFI, AND MUSIC.
WE CAN NOT GIVE A F*#5 RIGHT NOW!
I GUESS?
...
WHO CARES IF ANYONE JOINS US?
YEAH, WHAT THE HELL.
JUST DO YOUR THING AND PEOPLE WILL RESONATE.

LET'S DO IT.
tink
CHEERS MATE.
Ayee!
!
Tmp
Tmp Tmp
Ayee!
HEY.
HEY.
I'M SORRY.
ME TOO.
I GUESS WE'RE BOTH JERKS, HUH?
HEH, YEAH.
Fin.

IS SOMETHING WRONG...
"SIGH...
YOU PROMISED ME A FRIEND..
DID I NOT FULFILL...
IT WAS EXACTLY THE SAME...
YOU SAID IT WOULD BE DIFFERENT.
I WAKE UP...
AND THEY ARE GONE...
VERY WELL......

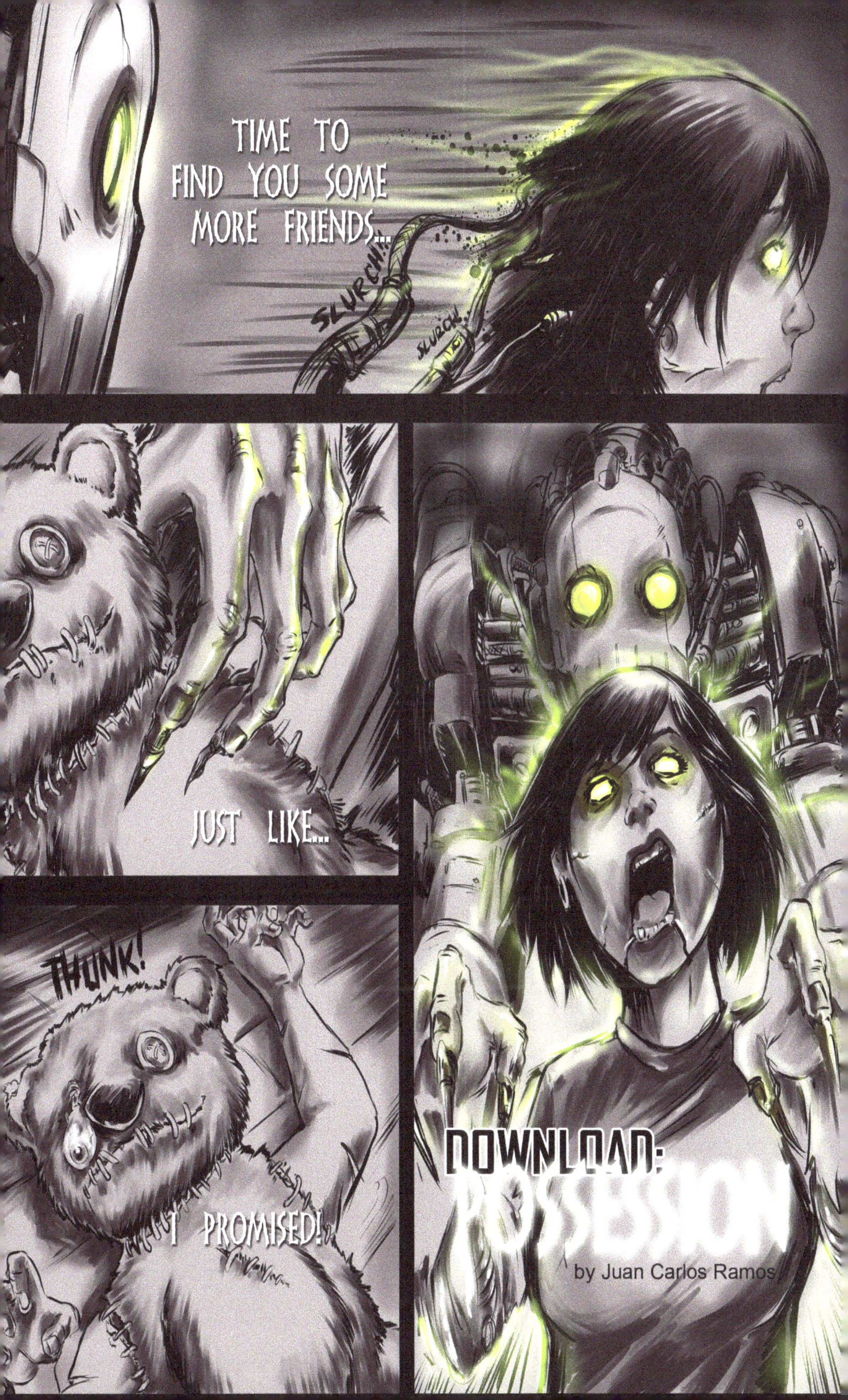

TIME TO FIND YOU SOME MORE FRIENDS...
SLURCH...
SLURCH...
SLURCH...

JUST LIKE...
THUNK!
I PROMISED!

DOWNLOAD: POSSESSION
by Juan Carlos Ramos

A SCREEN TO KILL FOR...
BATTLE ZONE
LAIR OF THE MINOTAUR
ZOMBIE NAZI HUNTER
VAMPIRE KILLER
ENTER
Written by: Greg Smith & Michael Tanner
Illustrated by: Meescha Dare

PLAYERS WEAR STATE OF THE ART HAPTIC SUITS WHICH SIMULATE REAL WORLD ACTION!!
CHOOSE FROM ONE OF THREE CURRENT IMMERSIVE GAME MAPS!!!
Dammit, are we the first ones here?
Does he really count though?
Theo's here.
So nice to see you Minnie, Jesse.
Am I too late? Did I miss the surprise?
What surprise?
I told you guys 7:30 sharp. You're supposed to already be inside.

HAPPY BIRTHDAY ANDREW!!!
I was here on time.
We need to go in. Our reservation is now.
So, will my massive muscles burst the seams on this suit?
They're one-size-fits-all, Kobe.
So how exactly does this work?
Sonni, are you playing with us or what?
Hmm? Yeah...
The suits have sensors on them. They affect your movement and let you know that you've been hit. It's a small shock.
They make it so you're skinned correctly in the game.
Skinned? Gross.
It means, you know, you're dressed right. Right?
I can put the goggles on myself you know.
goggles make it so you see the skins correctly. Even the space we're playing in is skinned.

Sorry, Jesse, I just wanted to help.
So which game are we playing? Zombie Nazis are way, way played out.
"Lair of the Minotaur"! Because it's my birthday and I fucking love mythology!
We know, sweetie.
So don't freak out, but the goggles lock on and you can't take them off before the game is over.
How do we know when the game is over?
One of us has to slay the minotaur, or we all get slain by the minotaur.
Two things I forgot to mention. One of us *is* the minotaur.
And, first to 10,000 points wins a free pizza.
Pizza?

PLAYERS TO YOUR STARTING POSITIONS!
Wait, so we don't start together?
Guys, which one's the minotaur? Is that the one with the snakes?
No you are thinking of the one with the lion dick.
Or get found by the minotaur.
No, we start scattered around the maze and have to find each other.
What? What does that even mean?
It's the one with the bull's head! Although classically it was a bull's body.
THE GAME WILL BE STARTING IN 3...
UP
THIS SIDE UP
2...1...
Hmmm.

Cool.
The monster stalks the maze.
The Minotaur, a frightening, selfish beast.
The monster will see death tonight.

This is sooo...
...weird.
What am I, a vampire? Are there vampires in this story? ...hope I'm a sexy vampire.
Minnie is a very pretty girl who always knew that fact. She knew she could get away with anything
Lame. Doesn't even feel like real fire.
She never had to work hard and could never bring herself to do it. That's why she found a way to cheat on her SATs. She thinks no one knows.
A monster knows...
YEAH! That's what I'm talking about!
But she won't be the monster's victim tonight.

I'M A WARRIOR!
YOU WANT A PIECE OF THIS!
He was always a decent athlete, but decent doesn't mean college athlete. Desperate, he tried anything to give himself a boost, but with drug testing, he had to choose a more exotic path
Oh poor Kobe, he doesn't know that his life has peaked.
THIS SIDE UP
THIS SIDE
I eat minotaurs for breakfast!!
No, Kobe. You eat tiger dick and black rhino horn for breakfast. The monster knows you'd have eaten dodo embro if you thought it would help you win the big game.
But this is not your night for punishment, either.

Lame.
Sonni...
Um, Hello?
Now is not her time to die.
Andrew's little sister...
I don't really know her. But she's not like Andrew. She seems self-centered. Probably stuck up.
Creeper.

Okay, don't want to get lost. I went left and then took twenty paces and turned right.
If the sword is in the center and the building itself is only...
We're getting close now.
Ari, Andrew's loyal girlfriend.
Ah, here we are.
Except for that one time she wasn't.
Nailed it!
And foolish Andrew forgave her, but the monster hasn't.

GOT YA!!
WAIT-
1000pts!
I WON!!
Good job, Sweetie.
Aw, man, I thought I was going to win.
If you won, why are we still in the game. Wasn't it supposed to end?
NEXT!!
1000pts!

1000pts!
1000pts!
1000pts!
1000pts!
Free pizza for life!!
Why isn't he getting up?
Remember, the suit keeps you from moving once you're dead. It locks up the joints.
Something doesn't seem right.
Oh...
click
That's fucked up.

The Minotaur...
HANDLE WITH CARE
OH MY GOD! YOU KILLED JESSE!!
You all killed Jesse. You killed Andrew's best friend.
HANDLE
I didn't even want to be here.
We didn't...
....
It was the game!

It was a malfunction or something! Don't blame me!!
POLICE
It's sad but...
They really should honor the free pizza we won, right? Like legally?
Sweetie-

Andrew...
I'm sorry, buddy.
I'm sorry you choose such awful people to be friends with.
Something like this should never have happened. You should be grateful for the time you did have with your friend.
I don't blame you if you have a hard time being around Ari and the others, considering what they did to Jesse.
Something like this should have happened much sooner. You should be grateful that you have a real friend like me looking out for you.
I'll be here for you.
Jesse... his sin... being Andrew's "best friend."
Sometimes when you want something in your life you have to make room for it.
Thanks, Theo. You're a true friend.
A Monster knows how to make room...

B IS FOR BEER

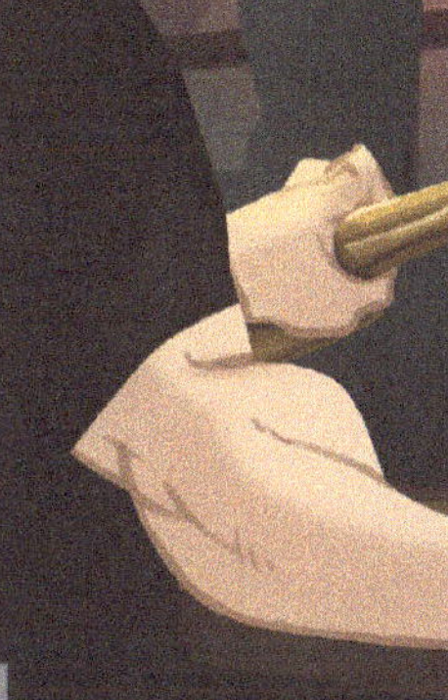

BROUGHT TO YOU TODAY BY...
THE LETTER S FOR *SCOTT BACHMANN* ON STORY AND LETTERING,
AND BY THE LETTER N FOR *NATE LOVETT* WHO DID ALL OF THE ART.

HEY. I NEED VODKA DOWN HERE.

KOWABUNGA!
YOU HAVE TWO GREAT EXAMPLES OF ME FAVORITE LETTER.

YEAH? WHAT OF IT.

ME WONDERING HOW MUCH TO GO IN ALLEY NOW AND ME SHOW YOU LETTER D.
I DON'T DO YOUR KIND.

ME KIND? ARE YOU A RACIST PERSON?
NO FREAK. I DON'T LIKE FUR IN MY TEETH.

THIS HAND JOCKEY BOTHERING YOU BABE?
HAND JOCKEY? AHA! YOU SIR ARE VERY MUCH A RACIST.
HOW ABOUT I RIP OUT YOUR STUFFING AND FEED IT TO YOU.
HEY. NONE OF THAT IN MY PLACE. HAVE A BEER ON THE HOUSE AND FORGET ABOUT IT.
AND MONSTER? IF YOU BOTHER MY PATRONS AGAIN I'LL THROW YOU OUT MYSELF.
WASTE IS BAD. SO ME HELPING.
YOU'RE SO LUCKY MY KID LOVED YOUR SHOW.

WHATEVER
JOE! J IS FOR JOE!
WHAT DOES HE OWE LARRY?
WHATEVER
NO JOE, IT NOT LAST CALL.
IT IS FOR YOU.
COME ON. LET'S GO.
WHO CALLED JOE HERE?
LARRY? DID YOU CALL JOE?
ME HATE YOU LARRY. CAN YOU SPELL ASSHOLE LARRY? ME CAN!
ME HATE YOU TOO JOE.
H-A-T-E Y-O-U J-O-E
YEAH, YEAH. JUST DON'T BARF ON THE SEATS THIS TIME.

ME COULD FIND MY HOME, STOP HERE. ME WALK.
AHHH.... NO.
YOU ALWAYS JERK JOE.
YOU'RE THE EXPERT. YOU'D KNOW.
ME PAY YOU BACK. NO WANT TO OWE YOU.
FORGET IT. I'M DOING GOOD. YOU WAIT 'TILL YOU'RE BACK ON YOUR FEET.
OH PLEASE. RUB IT IN.
I TOLD YOU TO TRY DIRECTING YEARS AGO.
I COULD STILL GET YOU IN AS MY ASSISTANT.
HAH. ME FUNNY. ME STAR. LETTER F THAT.
HEY JOE.
GUESS WHAT STARTS WITH LETTER G?
JEEZ! WHAT THE HELL?

YOU DON'T WANT TO DO THIS LETTER MONSTER! YOU HAVE SO MUCH TO LIVE FOR!
LIKE WHAT? SYNDICATION? ROYALTIES?
ME NO GOT THOSE. STUPID ACCOUNTANTS. THEY LOVE TO COUNT.
ONE. ONE ROYALTY STOLEN.
TWO. TWO BANK ACCOUNTS EMPTIED.
THREE. THREE FAT ACCOUNTANTS IN CAYMAN ISLANDS.
DON'T DO THIS! THINK OF THE NEWS TOMORROW.
THINK OF THE KIDS.
KIDS FORGET. KIDS FORGOT ME. KIDS NOT FORGET THIS THOUGH!
BANG
BAM!
GOOD ONE, HUH JOE?
ME STILL FUNNY, RIGHT JOE?
YEAH, YOU'RE STILL FUNNY.
NOW LET'S GET YOU HOME.
ADIOS!

Vengeance
VERDE CEM
D. GREENHILL
AND
L. KOHSE
PROPRIETORS

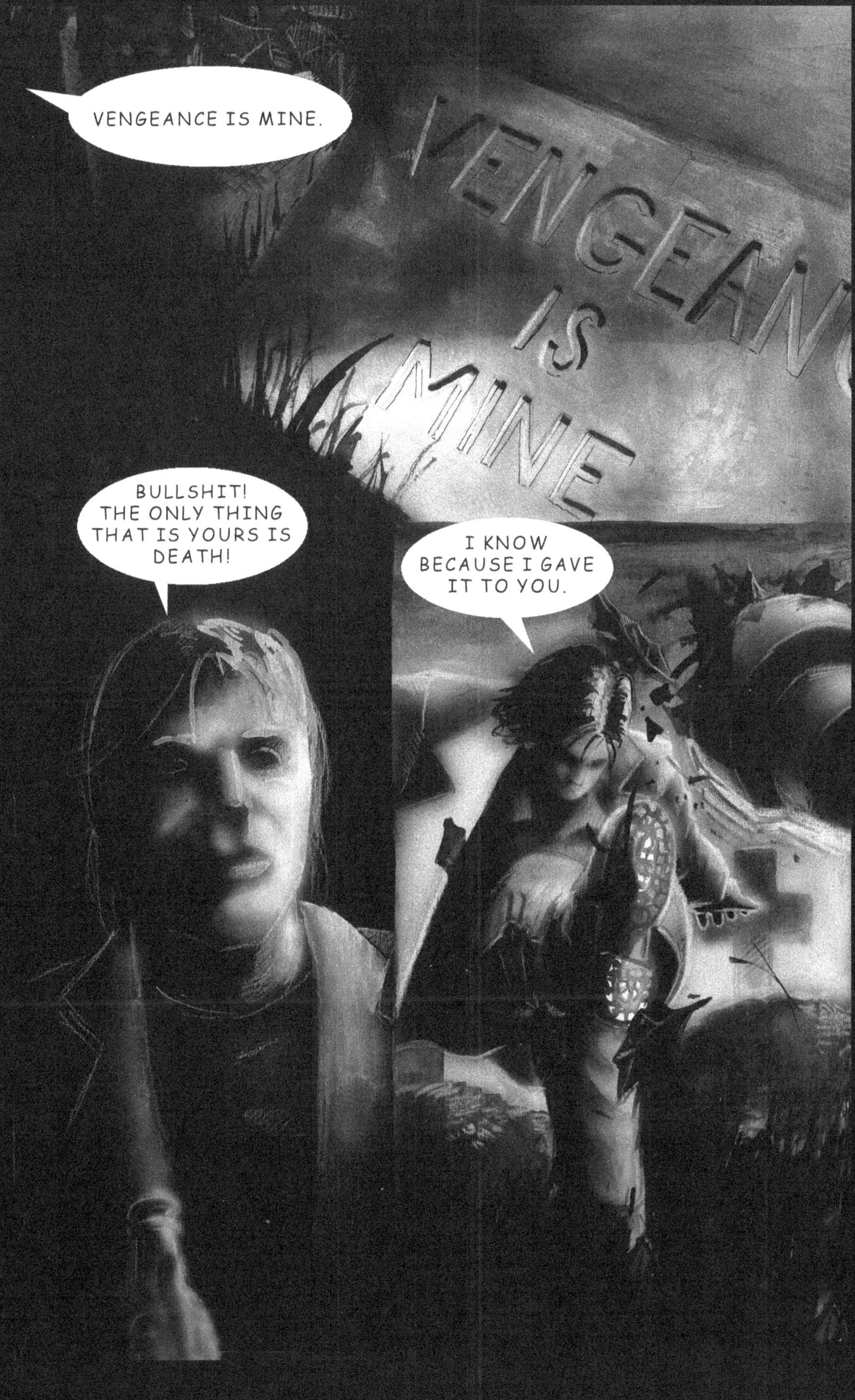

VENGEANCE IS MINE.
BULLSHIT! THE ONLY THING THAT IS YOURS IS DEATH!
I KNOW BECAUSE I GAVE IT TO YOU.

YOU'RE SUCH A BITCH!
I TOLD YOU NOT TO TELL THE PIGS ABOUT DRAGON'S OPERATIONS.

IT WAS
NOTHING PERSONAL
MY BROTHER.

IT WAS
ONLY BUSINESS.

WHAT THE FU...

OH SHIT!
VENGEANCE IS MINE!

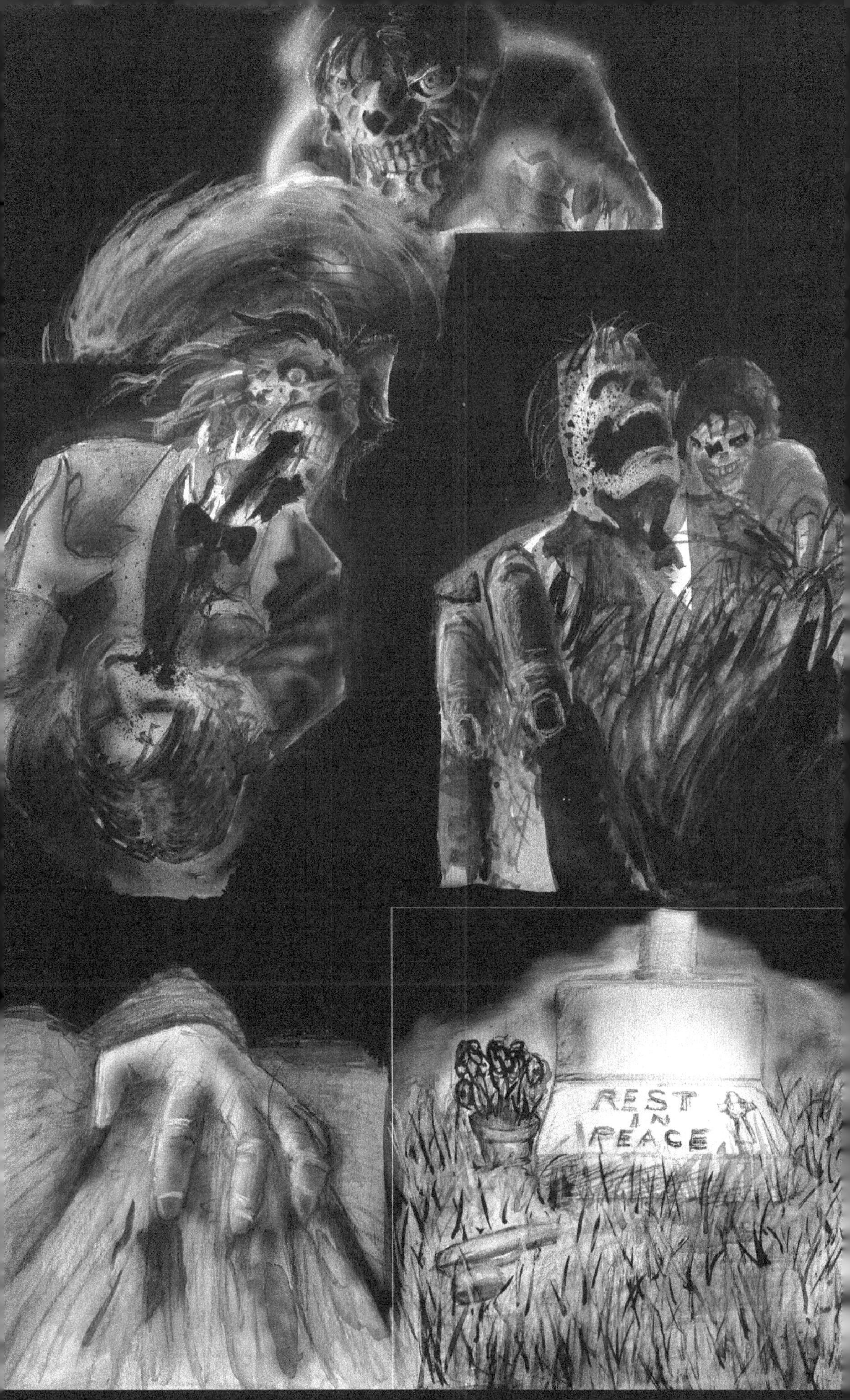
REST
IN
PEACE

Ah, the first day of school. A time for new beginnings, new friends, new... Actually, nothing about this place looks new.
Seriously, get somebody with a leaf blower over here.
MORRIS HEALY MEN'S ATHLETIC CLUB
Undeaducation
Created by Angela Heckman & Joe Ranoia
Story by Joe Ranoia
Visuals Cassidy Lee Phillips
Maybe it looks better on the inside?
CREEEEEEEEEEEEEK!
SLAM!
Nope...it's a dump.

Kids,
get to class.
Yes, Mr. Jove.
Welcome to Canny Valley High!
It's gonna be a long year.

We can't judge our undead students until we shuffle a mile in their shoes!
They're not evil. In fact, once socialized, they're quite normal...mostly.
Addie, as Hall Monitor you have to stop these kids cutting from class on your watch.
No jaw??
Alba de los Muertos, Canny Valley Principal
RRR... UNG..ERRRRRR. UUUUNNNNNNNG
Yes, they smell funny and try to eat people sometimes, but everyone has their faults.
I know there are a lot of them, but you have to get their names and report them.
AAAAANNNNNGGGGG.... HHUUUUUUUUURRRRRRRR
I agree.
Blech!
A school like this can be the bridge that fully brings them back to society.
Byron, what the hell am I doing here?
You, Juan, are the bridge between the world of the dead and the world of the living.
You've been talking to my mom.
It almost worked at Harvard, until the revolt and blood feast. So, instead of being that heavy-handed, we provide a nurturing environment where they can experience personal growth and feel safe.
Huh?
Well, she is the principal. Nice sneakers!
Never wear shoes you can't run for your life in... especially here.

World literature class, where kids can read and discuss the great literary works, without any political or ideological bias.
One of the great travesties in world literature is the blatant, wanton and inexcusable disregard for the undead.
OK, maybe a little bias. It's a liberal arts high school.
We need a proper voice to teach the living that we too have rights.
...that we are beings of character, with feelings, emotions, and great, unflappable dignity and class!
POP!
Shit.
CLICK!
Yeah, I'm leavin'.

Good morning everyone. This is our newest student, Juan de los Muertos.
Settle down. Settle down! Mr. Jove?
Fresh Meat!!
Is he alive?
I expect that you'll make Juan feel welcome!
Well, Juan, why don't you go take a seat?
Um...hi.
Is that Hot Principal's kid?
He's kinda cute!
Yes. Please.
I'll leave you to it, then!
Now, Where was I?
You were saying how people suck and zom...um...the living challenged are way better.
Oh boy.
Remember when I said this was going to be a long year? Well, that's assuming he lives through his first day!

A human? Really?
That's so awesome! How long do you think he lasts?
Three days.
Ooo eeeks (two weeks)
'Til lunch.
He's probably gonna be lunch!
Oh, I could eat him right up.
You see, now there's a few ways we can interpret this...none of them good...
Minutes later. I'm glad Juan has made it this long...
Hey, leave the kid alone!
I hate bullies.
Yeah! Um...wait, whose side are we on again?
Mr. Mathews, Mr. Venturini, are you causing trouble today?
But they were...
Now I'm sure you two have someplace to be, so get there.
Yes, Dean Rooney.
What are you looking at?
Just because you're not a rotting piece of filth doesn't mean you can get into fights with the rabble. I may not be here next time.
Now get to class!

Mom, get me out of here! They're chasing me all over the building!
I'll bet they were just being friendly.
They want to eat me.
Oh, stop overreacting. These kids are alone and scared.
I'm alone and scared. THEY are in a mob and have no feelings of any kind.
You miss my point. YOU have to be the bridge, Juan. You're an ambassador here.
What kind of message does it send if my own son wants to leave?
Here's the message. "I want to keep my son alive."
You can't promise anything.
This is far too important for you to be so selfish.
I promise you, nothing's going to happen. I know what I'm doing.
This is your locker combination. I've already put your textbooks there. You have lunch now. Grab your books for the afternoon and head to the cafeteria. It's a perfect place to make some new friends.
You know, none of this is gonna bring him back.

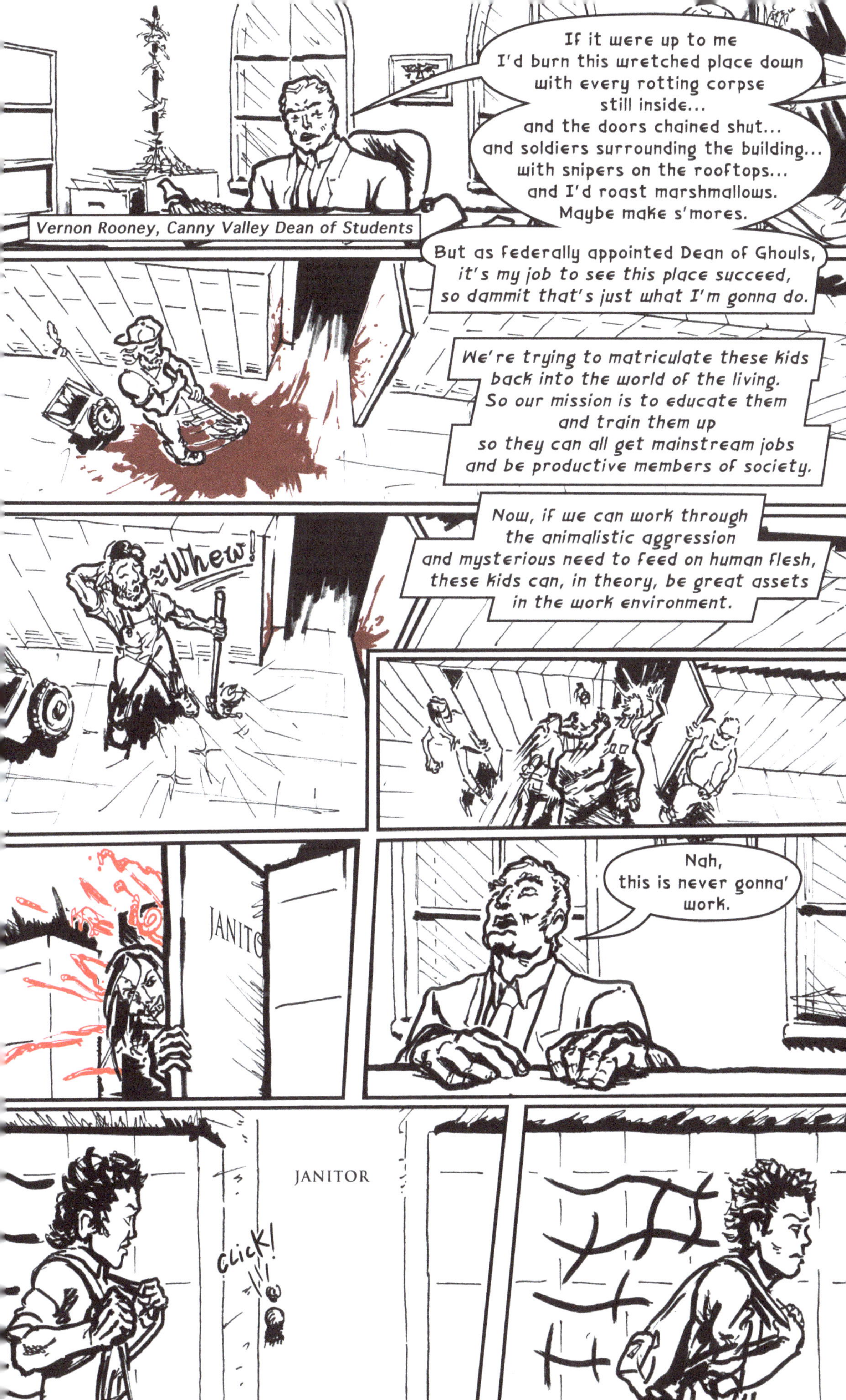

If it were up to me I'd burn this wretched place down with every rotting corpse still inside... and the doors chained shut... and soldiers surrounding the building... with snipers on the rooftops... and I'd roast marshmallows. Maybe make s'mores.
Vernon Rooney, Canny Valley Dean of Students
But as federally appointed Dean of Ghouls, it's my job to see this place succeed, so dammit that's just what I'm gonna do.
We're trying to matriculate these kids back into the world of the living. So our mission is to educate them and train them up so they can all get mainstream jobs and be productive members of society.
Now, if we can work through the animalistic aggression and mysterious need to feed on human flesh, these kids can, in theory, be great assets in the work environment.
Whew!
JANITO
Nah, this is never gonna' work.
JANITOR
CLICK!

Hi!
AAAAAAHHH!
Oh, sorry. I forgot I'm kinda' scary.
No it's not that.
Well, don't worry. I'm not gonna' eat your brains.
Good. But, I wasn't scared or anything.
You don't think I could eat your brains if I wanted them?
No way.
Then why'd you just jump like a little girl?
Whatever. Hey, what were you doing sneaking up on me like that anyway?
I just wanted to say 'hi' and let you know we're not all trying to eat you.
Oh. I get it. But, if you wanted to eat me, you could. Right?
Right!
Uh. Yeah, well I should go then. Where's the cafeteria?
Nom Nom Nom
I'll show you!
Thanks. I'm a little clumsy still... Sometimes.
You're fine.
So, if this was Degrassi High, this scene wouldn't be creepy. But, it's Canny Valley High, so it is.

Please don't use the word 'zombie'. My 'Living Challenged' students are mocked every day with terms like 'Zombie' and 'Stench.'
Rita Mortimer, Canny Valley Lit. Teacher/Undead Rights Activist
I suppose you've heard Principal de los Muertos use the 'shuffle a mile in their shoes' line. As if that isn't a stereotype?
What do you want? Rooney's up my butt because of you.
Sorry. But thanks for sticking up for me back there.
Whatever. Just be careful from now on. We're not your babysitters.
So, you two gonna sit or what?
I'm Larry. I'll try not to bite. No promises though.
Munch!
Munch!
Munch!
Munch!
Munch!
Munch!
These kids...These kids will never grow any older, than they are now. They won't have families and watch their children grow up.
No. They will eventually rot. And so will I. And that's the truth. Go shuffle a mile in those shoes!
And yet, these kids ARE here. Working hard, fighting the urge to feast and pursuing their dreams just like anybody else!
Hey...Why do they serve so much caramel corn here? It's not Halloween or anything.
Cuz it's yummy!
What did she say?
She said "high fructose corn syrup".
Ung rrrttooorrrssshhh errrrn shhherrrraaaa.
It slows down the rotting and curbs our need to eat...um...people. Nobody knows why.
Without it, we'd swallow you right up! Wouldn't that just be terrible?
See you around, Hot Stiff!
Huh? Do you mean "Hot Stuff"?
Not in our world.
Of course, some of them are still a little scary. But we can't all be saints, now can we?

One of the difficulties I face that other guidance counselors don't, is that occasionally my students try to eat me.
But if we focus on them, I think that the problems these kids face are really no different from those of any other teenager.
Well...Maybe a little different.
Byron Jove, Canny Valley Guidance Counselor
Every class??? Really!!??? Don't you guys have study hall or something??
Sorry, I didn't see you there...
Sorry. Habit.
Bad habit. Don't do that again.
Never.
I promise.
But I could if I wanted to! Now walk me to class.
Oh, what the hell... Sure.
And carry my books.
Don't push it!

A little while later.
Oh don't get me wrong, I want Juan to make friends. But he shouldn't lead her on.
What if he is interested?
When she finds out he's not interested,
it could hurt her feelings. ...I hope she CAN feel.
Teaching The Problem Child
Well, I made it through the first day, anyway. All in all it wasn't so bad. In Lit Class I learned living people suck, I discovered three new smells, I have a new appreciation for candy corn...
What? In her? Oh please. She's a Zombie for God's sake.
Why are you takin' the hearse to Z-Town?
I'm gonna' go see my dad.
Like, your dad's in Z-Town?
He's a "volatile." Too violent for rehabilitation
Oh, I'm so sorry.
...I made some friends, I think...or at least I met a few kids that don't want to eat me...
...I didn't die. I think any day you don't die is probably a good day.
And now I gotta' do it all again...
Come on, Hot Stiff!
Sit next to me!
Last thing we need is him having friends.
They're not friends. They're zombies. And we'll make sure they eat him alive.
...Tomorrow.
DEDDER IS BEDDER
DEAD LIVES MATTER
LIKE DEATH
DECAY IS BEAUTIFUL
KEEP THE DEAD BURIED
BLAME OBAMA!
LIVING POWER
That's one whole day of "Undeaducation" in the books!
Story: Joe Ranoia
Art: Cassidy Lee Phillips

MILLENNIALS AND DRAGONS BY NICOLAS TOURIS.
ADVENTURERS! WELCOME TO MY HUMBLE-

HONOOOR!

SWING!
WHAT THE HELL, MAN?

WHOA, DUDE, NOT COOL!

NOT... WHAT? I'M JUST GETTING RID OF THE GOBLIN, LOOK AT ALL THE LOOT HE HAS!

WHAAAAAAT.
DUDE HAVEN'T YOU LEARNED ANYTHING FROM UNDERTALE? JUST BECAUSE YOU'RE IN THE MONSTER MANUAL DOESN'T MEAN YOUR LIFE DOESN'T MATTER.

I SEE... SO ALL LIVES MATTER!

FELLOW ADVENTURERS!
I'M LOOKING FOR BRAVE COMPANIONS TO-

OH.
THE END.

GHOUL
Script & art ~ Alexander Yakimov
Inks & colors ~ Saint Yak
Lettering ~ HdE
WE'RE LATE. AGAIN.
CAW!

ANOTHER ONE.
LOOK AT THE CORPSE. IS IT ALL RIGHT?
NO. IT'S SHATTERED APART. ALL THAT'S LEFT ARE THE BONES - AND NOT ALL OF 'EM, EITHER.
IT WAS DUG NOT SO LONG AGO. THE BASTARD IS HERE. ACT WITH CAUTION.
THAT'S ODD...
WHAT?
THIS IS THE SECOND CEMETERY IN TWO NIGHTS... FIFTEEN GRAVES. AND THE BODIES WERE ONLY EATEN IN THREE OF THEM.
ALL THE GRAVES HE'S DESECRATED ARE UNMARKED. THAT'S NO ACCIDENT.
I STILL DON'T GET IT...
THE BEAST'S LOOKING FOR SOMETHING. HE'S NOT JUST SOME MINDLESS UNDEAD CREATURE. THERE'S SOMETHING ELSE...

GUYS - THERE'S SOMETHING HERE!
GOOD JOB.
RIP THIS SHIT APART!

JESUS... THAT WAS IT, RIGHT?
WHAT ELSE DO YOU THINK COULD DIG A HUGE PIT LIKE THIS WITH ITS BARE HANDS?
FAST BASTARD...
LOOK SHARP - IT COULDN'T HAVE GOT FAR. DON'T GO ANYWHERE ALONE. THIS ISN'T YOUR AVERAGE GHOUL.
MAKES NO DIFFERENCE TO ME. COUPLE OF BULLETS AND THIS THING...

...WILL
BE DEAD.

AAARRGH!

SON OF A BITCH...
?
HE WAS MY BEST MARKS- MAN!
COME ON!
AGH--!
NO...

LEAVE ME ALONE!
HOW DID YOU-? WHAT THE HELL ARE YOU?!
BLAMM
AHKK!
THE LORD IS MY SHEPHERD, I LACK NOTHING.
HE REFRESHES MY SOUL. HE GUIDES ME ALONG THE RIGHT PATHS FOR HIS NAME'S SAKE.
HE MAKES ME LIE DOWN IN GREEN PASTURES. HE LEADS ME BESIDE QUIET WATERS.
EVEN THOUGH I WALK THROUGH THE DARKEST VALLEY, I WILL FEAR NO...
GUK--!
...EVIL.

NOW IT'S YOUR TURN TO PRAY!
FHUCC
AAAARRGH!

AHK!
KRAK
I FOUND YOU...
BY SMELL.

IT'S SO STRANGE... ALL THESE THINGS... GRAVES... DEAD MEN... MURDERS. NONE OF THESE THINGS SEEM SO TERRIFYING.
IT'S SCARIER TO THINK THAT, AFTER DEATH...
...WE WILL BE FORGOTTEN.
LIKE WE NEVER EXISTED.

I'LL MAKE SURE YOU'RE REMEMBERED.
NO LONGER BY MY SIDE BUT FOREVER IN MY HEART
REST IN PEACE, MY WIFE...
I HOPE I'LL SEE YOU... SOON.
THE END

1881.
JESUS SAVE ME!
MAMA, IT IS ME.
IT IS THE DEVIL, LORD! HE HAS COME DRESSED IN MY VERY OWN BODY TO ENTICE ME.
HE TEMPTS ME WITH MY YOUTH, SWEET JESUS.
MAMA, I AM YOUR DAUGHTER.
BACK, SATAN! I WILL NOT BE TAKEN BY YOUR KIND.
MAMA!
KNOCK KNOCK
WHO'S THERE?
LAST RITES
holland words
fisher pictures
cordes letters

OH... IT IS THE PRIEST OF THE IDOL.
WHERE IS YOUR MOTHER, CHILD?
IN BED. DYING.
NO.
NO?
YOU WOULD REFUSE YOUR MOTHER REDEMPTION?
SHE NEEDS NO REDEEMING.
WE ALL NEED GOD'S REDEMPTION.
PERHAPS. BUT WHOSE GOD?
THERE IS BUT ONE TRUE GOD.
HAVE YOU TALKED TO YOUR GOD RECENTLY? SEEN HIM?

AH, YOU ARE THE ONE NAMED FOR HER?

YES.

I HAVE HEARD THE TWO OF YOU WERE QUITE CLEVER

IN YOUNGER DAYS. YOU LOOKED SO MUCH ALIKE MARIE LAVEAU COULD BE IN TWO PLACES AT ONCE. NO WONDER THE HEATHEN WERE FOOLED.

THE ONLY HEATHEN ARE THOSE WHO LISTEN TO YOU.

BUT THEY BECOME SAVED. AS CAN YOU.

I CARRY ON MY MOTHER'S TRADITIONS AS WELL AS HER NAME.

YOU PRACTICE VOODOO?

OF COURSE. HAVE YOU NOT BEEN LISTENING?

I DID NOT REALIZE. GOD SAVE YOUR SOUL.

I DO NOT WANT YOUR GOD! WHY CAN'T YOU LET US BE? DO WE TRY AND FORCE OUR BELIEFS ON YOU?

YOU BELIEVE IN THINGS YOU CANNOT SEE!

YOU SHOULD NOT TREAT GOD'S OBJECTS IN SUCH A MANNER.
YOU HAVE NOT HEARD A WORD I HAVE SAID, HAVE YOU?

I ASKED IF YOU'VE SEEN YOUR GOD. WELL, I HAVE SEEN MINE!
THIS IS MY BELIEF, PRIEST!

WHAT?

NOOOO

YOU MAY DIE, MAMA, BUT MARIE LAVEAU THE VOODOO QUEEN SHALL LIVE.

SNAP

THE FEAR MONSTER

Now this is an awful thing.

Imagine a monster that makes you all queasy, sweaty, feverish, jangly,
icy-cold, and absolutely nauseated at the same time.

This is something that grips you below the eyes, drags its icy claws
into your cheekbones, and pulls you under in a crunching heap, sobbing
- not knowing what to do.

This is the monster that makes you feel absolutely stupid and immobile.

This is the Fear Monster.

You cannot see it, unsee it, feel it, unfeel it.

It is very so much there.

It very much makes you helpless and crying.

NORA TORA STUDIOS

I HAD ALWAYS WONDERED...
WHAT HAPPENED TO BUTTERFLIES WHEN THEY DIED...
:STORY BY ARTHUR BELLFIELD
: ART BY BLAIR ROSSI
: COLORS BY KEVIN GREEN

I MEAN
BEING A CATAPILLER FOR MOST OF YOUR LIFE IS COOL AND ALL

BUT...

WHAT'S THE POINT OF EMERGING FROM THE COCOON LIKE A SUPER MODEL...

IF YOU ONLY LIVE FOR SEVEN DAYS?!?

THEN AGAIN...
WHY AM I ALMOST NAKED WITHIN A FOREST MADE UP OF DREAMS?

...

MAYBE THE ANSWER TO BOTH QUESTIONS...

IS THAT THEY DON'T DIE AND I'M NOT REALLY NAKED AT LEAST PHYSICALLY.

HOWEVER, THERE ARE RIPPLES IN REALITY THAT HINT AT SOMETHING ELSE...
THEY SAY THAT ONCE BUTTERFLIES FADE FROM THIS REALITY THEY ARE BORN AGAIN!

FEAR
ROR!
Here at whydoirock.com we specialize in fear.
We've been burning cities for years!

But don't take my word for it!
See what actual, real life people have to say about our services!
Take Jerry Alvarez. He's a terrified little man, thanks to me!
BRAD

He's come again.

He's destruction.

We tried to fight him...
HA! HA!
HA! HA! HA!
HA!HA!
HA!HA
LOL!
HA!HA!
HA! HA!
HA!HA!
OH BOY!
HA!
HA!HA!
HA!HA!
HA!
BOOM!
RB

He's unstoppable.

He's inevitable.
OUCHIES!

All you can do is rebuild.

I don't even know why we try...

I try to pretend I'm not afraid.
I can't take it anymore!
Now hold on...
That's it!
All these Monsters and Other Scary Shit are driving me crazy!

I put on a brave face.

Sometimes I even believe myself.

I hope people don't see how scared I am.
Why don't you just leave us alone, you big bully!?

We're all scared.

We all know it.

We all refuse to say it.

Maybe that's how we keep going.

I think about it a lot.
I try not to.
It's hard.
Sometimes I think he's trying to tell us something...
ROAR!
GRUMBLE
ROR!!
SNARL-!

Jerry is a great guy, tho.

I pick on him a little. OK, a lot.

But he's alright.

Beers All gone?!

...

Anyway, there's tons more stuff to be afraid of!

Let's take a look!

We used to rule this world...

Now look at us...

There aren't too many of us these days.
I mean, we're awesome, I don't know how you humans did it.

Wait a minute... Are you seriously destroying our city because you think we killed you?
It was an asteroid!

What?! No... I mean... An asteriod, huh?
Whatever.

This is my ancestral home! And you're acting like no one lives here!

There are thousands of other living species trying to find a way to survive in this city, and you can't even name five, I bet!

Five? Easy...
Cats. Dogs. Seagulls.
...
Cats.
...
and uh...

But who cares about them anyway!
Only we matter!

See what I mean?

I care!
Finally, someone bigger and badder than you!

You know what that means?

I WIN!!

Huh. That didn't take long.
You humans...
It's just too easy!
Well, here's my last few thoughts...

zzzz
Fear is a funny thing
its every where
Some people can't handle their fear...
MANVILL
Some people thrive on it
LOCAL GIRL IN
TO CRASH
It isn't an easy thing to deal with...
But it rarely goes away on its own.
If you take action it doesn't
always go away

And often, it doesn't come back

Well... In the same form, anyway...

Although each time it rears its head...

You're a little more prepared.

Until facing your fear is just another part of life

Fear is different for everyone

Some people don't seem to fear anything

CLICK!

While others seem to be afraid of everything

Some tough guys can't handle spiders.

Some people have trideskaphobia.

(That's fear of the number 13)
13!

A lot of people are afraid of the unknown.

That doesn't bother me any.

We come from the unkown, you know.
NOoooooo!!

Fear is a funny, after all...

Well, that's it.

...

What?!

I've wrapped up this whole fear thing.

Pretty handidly, too!

Only one thing left to do.
Ha! Ha!
HA! Ha!
Ha! Ha!
Bwa! Ha! Haa! Ah!
HAHA! Ha! HA!
Ha!
Ha!
BRAD

THE BOOGEYMAN
SCRIPT CHRISTIAN DOUGLAS
PENCILS AND INKS IVAN SARNAGO
THE FIRST VICTIM I SAW WAS IN THE WOODS. WELL, TECHNICALLY IT WASN'T JUST ONE. LATER, WE DISCOVERED IT WAS ONLY HER FACE SEWN TO ANOTHER MAN'S SKULL. BUT I'M GETTING AHEAD OF MYSELF.
"MR DREBIN, JUST TELL ME WHAT YOU REMEMBER. LET ME ASSURE YOU I'M NOT INTERROGATING YOU. WHATEVER YOU SAY FOLLOWS THE PATIENT/DOCTOR CONFIDENTIALITY CLAUSE. PLEASE RELAX."
"PLEASE CALL ME CARL. I'M JUST A LITTLE NERVOUS. THIS IS THE FIRST TIME THEY'VE MADE ME TALK TO A SHRINK. SORRY, YOU PROBABLY DON'T LIKE THAT NICKNAME."
"YOUR EVALUATION SHOWS ERRATIC BEHAVIOUR, LIEUTENANT. ALWAYS ON THE PRECINCT. YOUR WIFE EVEN CALLED WORRIED TO SEE IF YOU'RE STILL ALIVE."

"YEAH I KNOW... I'VE TAKEN THIS CASE WAY TOO PERSONAL. BUT HAVE YOU READ WHAT HE DID TO THAT POOR GIRL? THAT'S SOMETHING THAT NEVER WEARS OFF."

"IT TOOK US MORE THAN AN HOUR TO GET A ROUGH INDICATION OF WHERE THE BODY WAS. WELL...WHAT WAS LEFT OF IT."

"WHEN WE RECEIVED THE CALL FROM THE GUYS AT THE PRECINCT, WE ONLY HAD A WACKO SCREAMING AGAIN AND AGAIN: 'BOBO TOOK HER! BOBO TOOK HER!' "

"YOU SEE DOC, AS A HOMICIDE DETECTIVE YOU LOOK AT A LOT OF FUCKED UP SHIT - STABS, HEADSHOTS, BULLETS EVERYWHERE. YOU TAKE THAT FOR GRANTED WHEN THEY GIVE YOU THE BADGE. BUT DECAPITATION? GEEEEZ... THAT IS A WHOLE DIFFERENT LEVEL OF FUCKED UP!"
"UNITS WERE DEPLOYED TO CONTAIN THE AREA. AS I STARTED TO EXAMINE THE SCENE, I NOTICED THERE WASN'T ANY BLOOD, WHICH IS ODD. EVEN IF THE BODY WAS KILLED ELSEWHERE THERE'S ALWAYS A LITTLE BLOOD."
"WHEN THE FORENSIC TEAM SHOWED UP WITH THEIR LAMPS AND SHIT MY SUSPICIONS WERE CONFIRMED. NOTHING ON THE HEAD, NOTHING ON THE SCENE, NOTHING ON THE ROAD. THEY EVEN TOOK LEAVES TO EXAMINE FOR DNA AT THE LAB..."
"NO HAIR, NO EYELASHES, NO SMALL OBJECTS, NO PIECES OF CLOTHING, AND OF COURSE, NO WEAPONS. NOTHING!!"

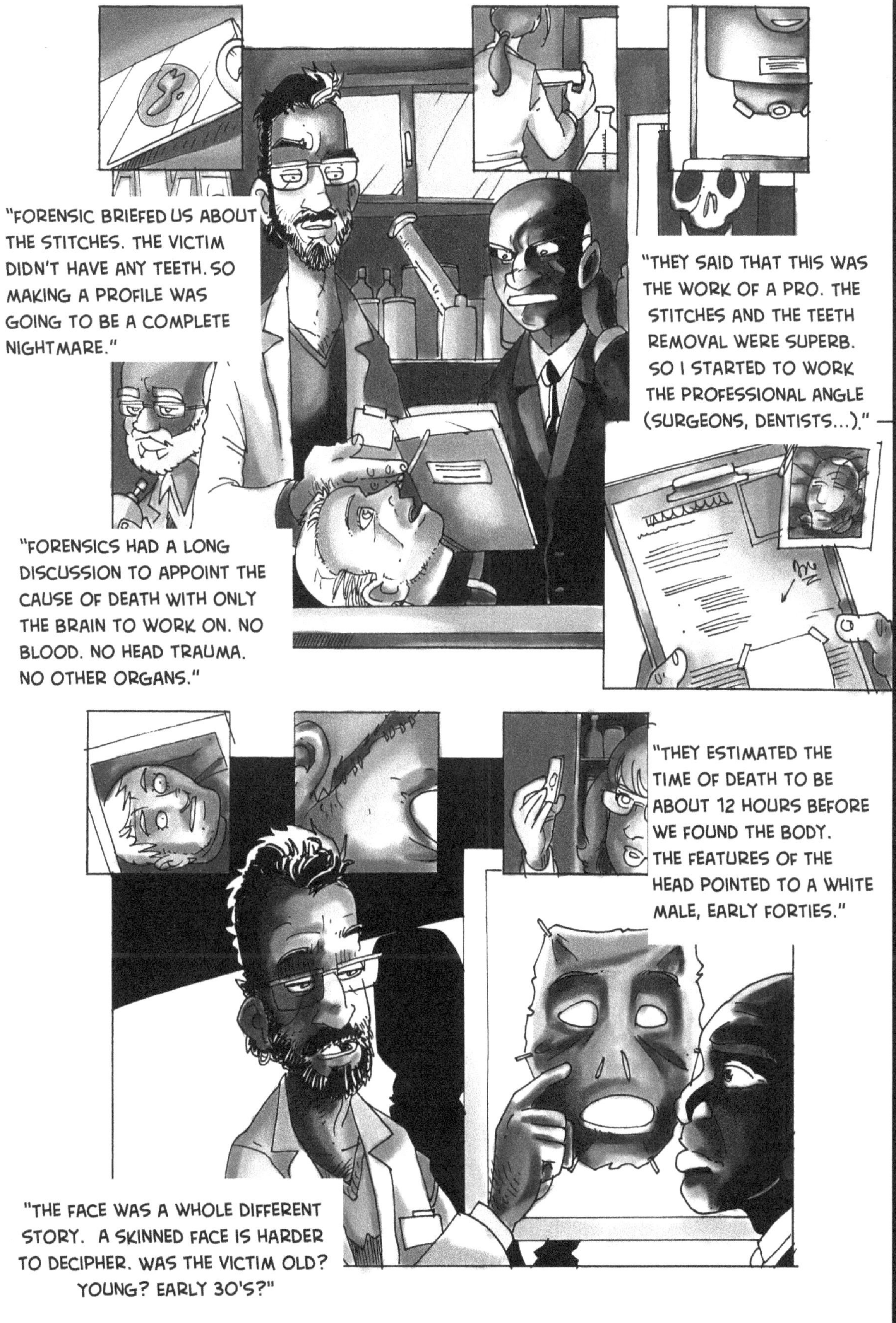

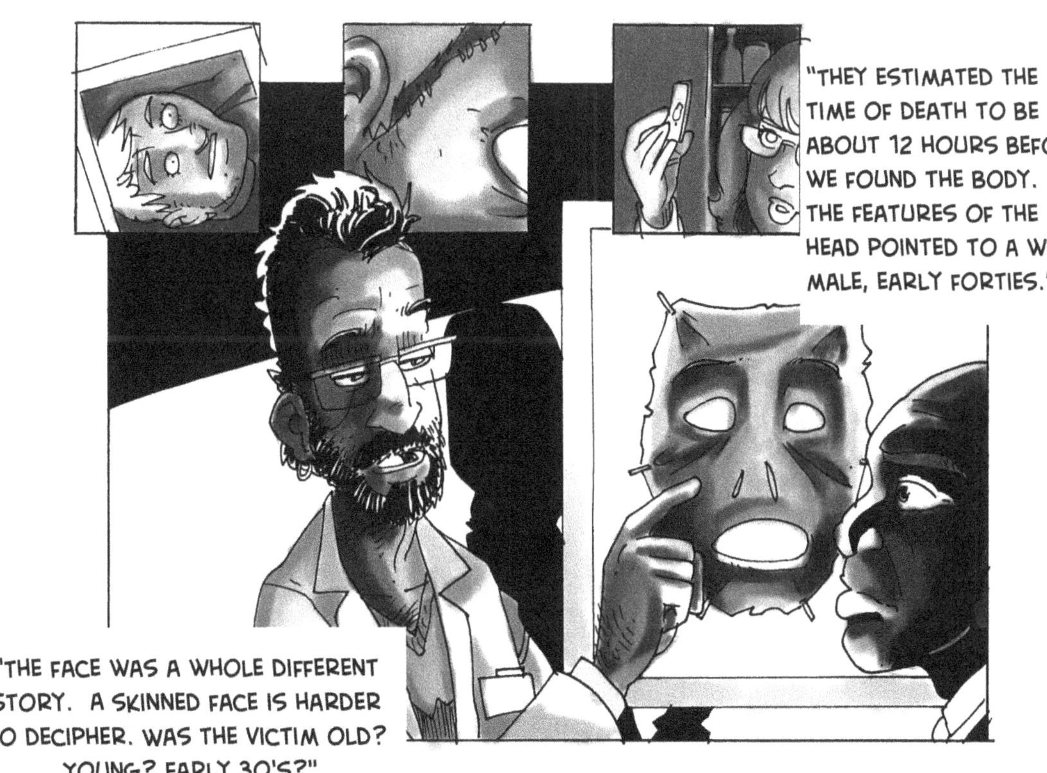

"FORENSIC BRIEFED US ABOUT THE STITCHES. THE VICTIM DIDN'T HAVE ANY TEETH. SO MAKING A PROFILE WAS GOING TO BE A COMPLETE NIGHTMARE."
"THEY SAID THAT THIS WAS THE WORK OF A PRO. THE STITCHES AND THE TEETH REMOVAL WERE SUPERB. SO I STARTED TO WORK THE PROFESSIONAL ANGLE (SURGEONS, DENTISTS...)."
"FORENSICS HAD A LONG DISCUSSION TO APPOINT THE CAUSE OF DEATH WITH ONLY THE BRAIN TO WORK ON. NO BLOOD. NO HEAD TRAUMA. NO OTHER ORGANS."
"THEY ESTIMATED THE TIME OF DEATH TO BE ABOUT 12 HOURS BEFORE WE FOUND THE BODY. THE FEATURES OF THE HEAD POINTED TO A WHITE MALE, EARLY FORTIES."
"THE FACE WAS A WHOLE DIFFERENT STORY. A SKINNED FACE IS HARDER TO DECIPHER. WAS THE VICTIM OLD? YOUNG? EARLY 30'S?"

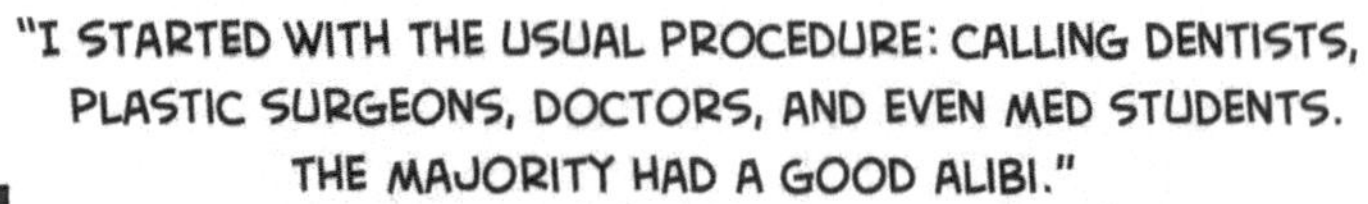

"THE HEAD OF THE FORENSIC DEPARTMENT, DR.FEELGOOD, AS CAUSE OF DEATH, STATED 'A HEAD NEEDS A BODY TO LIVE PS: CALL THE PSYCHIC LINE' "

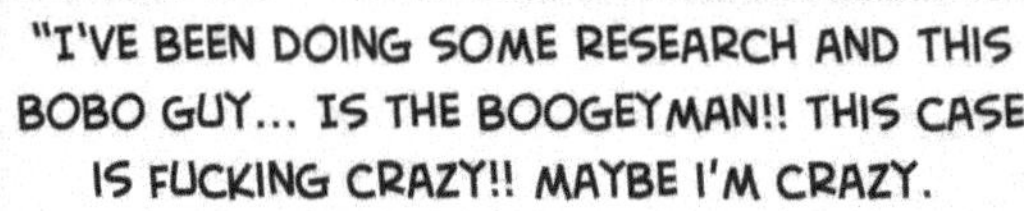

"AFTER INTERVIEWING EVERYONE I WENT TO SPEAK TO MY OLD FRIEND, DR. WHITE. HE WANTED TO EXAMINE THE HEAD, SO I SNUCK HIM INTO THE MORGUE. THE STITCHES WERE ANOTHER DEAD END. AFTER SOME QUICK EXAMINATION, HE TOLD ME THERE WAS SOMETHING ODD ABOUT THE DECEASED'S EXPRESSION."
I'M NOT THAT KIND OF DOCTOR, LIEUTENANT.
I TOLD YOU TO CALL ME CARL.
ALLRIGHT CARL. I CAN'T PRESCRIBE YOU ANYTHING DIRECTLY, BUT I WORK WITH A PSYCHIATRIST. DON'T WORRY.

"YOU SEE, IN THE MAJORITY OF VIOLENT DEATHS, THE VICTIM TENDS TO SHOW LOGICAL STRESSED EXPRESSIONS. THE NERVES ARE ALWAYS PARTICULARLY STIFF, BUT THIS GUY'S NERVES WERE INTACT. HE LOOKED CALM, AND WE DIDN'T SEE ANY SIGNS OF A FIGHT. SO... HE KNEW HIS AGGRESSOR - THAT'S ALSO VERY COMMON, BUT WITH HIM BEING A JOHN DOE WHO AM I GOING TO ASK?"

"WHEN THE SECOND HEAD COMBOS APPEARED, I CALLED THE FEDS. THEY DESTROYED ME WITH DATA. EVERY YEAR IN AMERICA THERE ARE MORE THAN 120,000 REPORTS OF MISSING PERSONS. 94% ARE CLEARED. SO MORE THAN 7,000 HUMAN BEINGS NEVER REAPPEAR. SOMETIMES THESE DISAPPEARANCES MAKE SENSE: SOME PEOPLE WANT TO VANISH. CRIMINALS OR ANYONE TOO FED UP WITH THEIR ROUTINE OR MAYBE SOMEONE WHO TOOK HIS LIFE IN A HARD PLACE TO FIND"

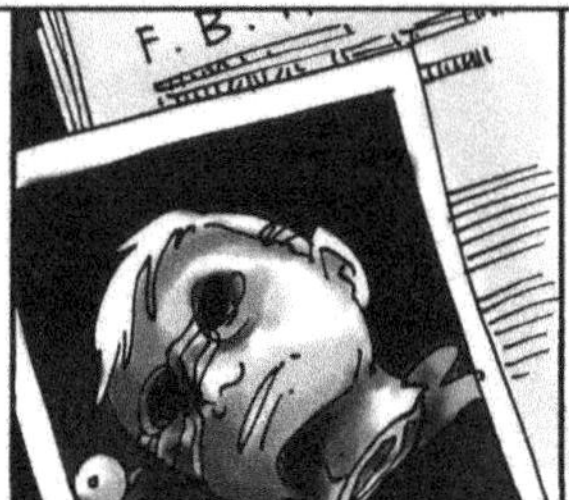

"BUT SOMETIMES PATTERNS EMERGE. SOMEONE OPENS A SHAFT OR A LAKE IS DRAINED AND WE HAVE BODIES ALL OVER THE PLACE. I MENTIONED THE DETAILS TO AGENT MCNULTY FROM THE SERIAL KILLER DIVISION, BUT HE DIDN'T HAVE ANYTHING RECENT ON SKINNING OR BEHEADINGS. NO SEXUAL CONNOTATIONS, OR FULL BODIES, I WAS STARTING TO THINK MAYBE THIS GUY WAS A VAMPIRE OR THE CHUPACABRA!"

"THEN ANOTHER FED CALLED ME. THIS TIME WITH INFO ON BEHEADINGS. HE'S PART OF THE DEA, AND THE SCENES WERE NOT THE SAME. YOU SEE... THE CARTEL LEAVES EVERYTHING THERE, IN PLAIN SIGHT. SO, I STARTED ALL OVER AGAIN. THERE MUST BE SOMETHING I'M MISSING. I WENT THROUGH THE REPORTS AND STUDIED ALL THE MISSING PERSONS CASES – A PATTERN SHOULD EMERGE... AND THEN IT HIT ME...IT HAS TO BE SOMEONE HARD TO GET LIKE A COP WITH MEDICAL SKILLS..."

SO WHAT ARE YOU EXPECTING FROM THESE SESSIONS, CARL?

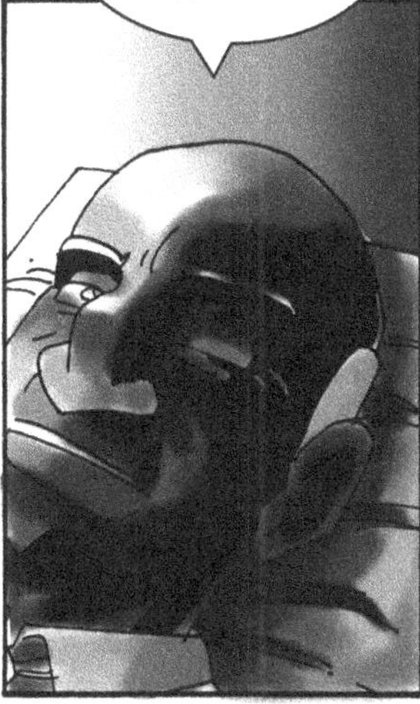

I JUST WANT TO GET SOME SLEEP, DOC. YOU KNOW, TO CLEAR MY HEAD.

THERE ARE SEVERAL THINGS WE COULD DO. LET'S TRY THIS FOR A SECOND. I WANT YOU TO CLOSE YOUR EYES AND BREATHE DEEPLY...NOW I WANT YOU TO LISTEN TO MY VOICE. I'M GOING TO GUIDE YOU TO A PLACE YOU WILL NOT BELIEVE...

PREETTY!!

SOME MONTHS LATER...
SO, MRS B. CAN YOU HELP ME TO GET SOME SLEEP?
FOR SURE! YOU WOULDN'T BELIEVE WHAT ALL MY YEARS OF EXPERIENCE HAVE MADE ME CAPABLE OF...
THE END?

THE LEGEND OF THE WHITE LADY

A YOUNG MAN CRYING ALONE.

JOHN SEEMED TO HAVE IT ALL.
HE WAS A SUCCESSFUL CARPET MAKER...
WHO HAD MARRIED HIS CHILDHOOD SWEETHEART, MAGDALENE.

BUT AS THE YEARS WENT BY, THEIR UNION FAILED TO PRODUCE A CHILD AND THEIR LOVE GREW DIM.

HE FOUND HIMSELF WISHING FOR A WOMAN WHO LOVED HIM AND COULD BEAR HIM A SON.

AND AS HE WISHED HE FORGOT TO SAY "BY THE GRACE OF GOD," WHICH YOU SHOULD ALWAYS SAY IF THAT'S THE AVENUE BY WHICH YOU WANT YOUR WISH FULFILLED.

PERHAPS IT WAS HIS TEARS, BUT THIS WAS THE FIRST MAN MARY HAD EVER SEEN SHE DID NOT WANT TO KILL.

THEY WALKED AND TALKED AND LAUGHED, AND MADE PLANS TO MEET THE NEXT NIGHT.

SOON THEY WERE IN LOVE, BUT WHAT TO DO ABOUT MAGDALENE?

JOHN HIRED MARY TO DO HOUSEKEEPING IN THE EVENINGS.

THUS, MARY GAINED HER CONFIDENCE.
ONE RAINY NIGHT, THEY WENT FOR A WALK.

AND MARY PUSHED MAGDALENE INTO AN ONCOMING TRAM!

BUT AS SHE DID...
THE LONG DRESS THAT COVERED HER HOOVES WAS CAUGHT UNDER THE WHEELS!

WHEN THE BODIES WERE FOUND THEY BOTH APPEARED QUITE DEAD.
BUT THE BAOBHAN SITH IS A CREATURE THAT CANNOT DIE.
JOHN COULDN'T BEAR THE THOUGHT OF NEVER SEEING MARY AGAIN.
HE HIRED A SCULPTOR TO CAPTURE HER LIKENESS IN A STATUE ABOVE THEIR GRAVES.

DURING THE PROCESS THEY DISCOVERED HER DEFORMITY.
HE INSTRUCTED THE SCULPTOR TO INCLUDE THE ABERRATION THAT HE MIGHT REMEMBER HER AS SHE WAS.

THUS SHE LIVES NOW...
THE WHITE LADY OF THE SOUTHERN NECROPOLIS.
YOU CAN GO AND SEE HER.
BUT WHEN THE RAIN HAS MADE THE GROUND SOFT...
DON'T STAND TOO CLOSE.

DON'T GET LOST LOOKING IN HER EYES...
WISHING FOR THE REMEDY TO A BROKEN HEART, YOUNG HUNTER.

FOR IT IS A SHALLOW GRAVE, THE WHITE LADY CAN SMELL YOU, AND SHE IS SO VERY...
HUNGRY!

NIGHTWALKER

ART AND STORY © MARY BELLAMY 2016

...DO...
...THAT...
Ooooooo oooooO
BITE!
WHAT THE HE-
SPLAT
OH CRA-
CHOMP!
MUNCH!
BITE!
TEAR!
RIP!
CHEW!
CRUNCH!
I HATE WALKING HOME ALONE...
BURP!
EN

One Last Tear

written by Nick Dean
Art by Daniele Serra

I CAN'T BELIEVE YOU'RE ACTUALLY GOING TO GO IN THERE.
ME? I'M NOT GOING IN, YOU ARE!
YOU SAID YOU WANTED TO FIND OUT WHAT'S IN THERE!
YES! THAT'S WHY I BROUGHT YOU, ALEX! AND I EXPECT YOU TO TELL ME ALL ABOUT IT.
I CAN'T BELIEVE YOU DRAGGED US ALL THE WAY OUT HERE JUST TO WUSS OUT!
COME ON! SOMEBODY'S GOT TO GO IN THERE!
RELAX LOSERS. I'LL DO IT.
NO MARA, ONE OF US WILL DO THIS.
WHY CAN'T I DO IT?

BECAUSE YOU'RE A...UM... I'M STOPPING NOW.
A WHAT?! A GIRL? WELL UNLESS YOU CAN GROW A PAIR IN THREE SECONDS, I'M GOING IN.
WHOA!

I HAVE A FEELING YOU'RE NOT GETTING LAID FOR A WHILE.
IT'LL BE AT LEAST A WEEK.

45 MINUTES LATER.

I'M STARTING TO THINK WE SHOULD GO IN AND FIND HER.

I'M SERIOUS! I THINK WE NEED TO...

ARE YOU KIDDING?! IF SHE DIDN'T MAKE IT OUT, THAT'S JUST ONE MORE REASON WE SHOULDN'T GO IN THERE!

AAHHH!

MARA!

RUN!

WHAT?!

RUN!!!

OKAY, OKAY. THIS SHOULD BE GOOD ENOUGH.

WE CAN REST HERE FOR A MINUTE.

WHAT DID YOU SEE? WHAT WAS IN THERE?

YOU BETTER NOT BE SCREWING WITH US!

I'M NOT! I SWEAR! LISTEN, THIS IS WHAT HAPPENED...

THE PLACE GAVE ME THE CREEPS FROM THE INSTANT I SET FOOT INSIDE.
IT GAVE ME A CHILL, LIKE THE BUILDING ITSELF WAS A GHOST!
I COULDN'T STOP IMAGINING WHAT ATROCITIES MIGHT HAVE BEEN COMMITTED IN EVERY CORNER OF THIS CHURCH.
I KNOW IT WAS BUILT TO BE A HOUSE OF GOD, BUT IT JUST DIDN'T FEEL LIKE IT TO ME.
I SPENT SOME TIME ON THE GROUND FLOOR LETTING MYSELF GET SPOOKED BY A LOT OF STUPID LITTLE THINGS BECAUSE I WAS TRYING TO AVOID THE THING THAT REALLY SCARED ME.
BUT EVENTUALLY, CURIOSITY GOT THE BETTER OF ME.
EACH STEP FELT LIKE IT WAS ABOUT TO GIVE WAY. AND EACH STEP SURPRISED ME BY SUPPORTING MY WEIGHT.
GRRrrrRrrrr!!
A DOG?!

WE RAN ALL THIS WAY, LIKE FRIGHTENED CHILDREN, OVER A DOG?
NO, DUMBASS, WE WEREN'T RUNNING FROM THE DOG. NOW SHUT UP AND LISTEN.

PEDRO!
SIT!

IS SOMEONE THERE? PLEASE HELP ME! PLEASE!
PEDRO! COME HERE BOY!
FOLLOW MY DOG, HE'LL SHOW YOU WHERE I AM.

UH...HEL... HELLO?
THANK GOODNESS! SOMEONE IS OUT THERE!
I'VE BEEN LOCKED IN HERE FOR WHAT SEEMS LIKE AN ETERNITY.
YOU HAVE TO FIND THE KEYS. THEY SHOULD BE NEARBY.

I'VE GOT THEM.

I CANNOT THANK YOU ENOUGH. AND WHAT A SIGHT TO BEHOLD! MY RESCUER IS SUCH A PRETTY GIRL.
I NEVER THOUGHT A PRETTY GIRL WOULD STIR SUCH BITTERSWEET EMOTIONS IN ME.
WHAT DO YOU MEAN?
YES, PEDRO, YES. IT'S BEEN A VERY LONG TIME.
I'VE LOST THE USE OF MY LEGS.
YOU MAY HAVE UNLOCKED THE DOOR TO MY PRISON, BUT A GIRL LIKE YOU COULDN'T POSSIBLY CARRY ME THROUGH THAT DOORWAY.
BECAUSE I'M A GIRL?
WELL...
DON'T SAY ANYTHING THAT WILL GET YOU INTO MORE TROUBLE.
MY GENDER DOESN'T MAKE ME WEAK. I'LL CARRY YOU THROUGH THAT DOOR, DOWN THE STAIRS AND OUT TO YOUR FREEDOM.

WHAT IS YOUR NAME?
MARA.

I AM VERY PLEASED TO MEET YOU MARA. I BELIEVE YOU ARE CAPABLE OF WHAT YOU SAY.
IT HAS BEEN A LONG TIME SINCE I HAVE HAD FAITH IN ANOTHER PERSON. THANK YOU. I AM MARCOS.
WAIT, WAIT, WAIT...

FIRST IT WAS A DOG, NOW IT'S A CRIPPLE?
DID YOU ACTUALLY SEE ANYTHING SCARY?
MAYBE IF YOU COULD SHUT YOUR MOUTH, I'D GET TO THAT.

SO, ANYWAY...I HOISTED MARCOS UP ON MY BACK AND WE MADE OUR WAY TOWARD THE STAIRS.

YOU ARE TRULY A WOMAN OF GREAT STRENGTH.
THAT'S KIND OF YOU TO SAY, BUT I'M ALREADY STARTING TO GET TIRED.

HAH!
WHOA!
CAREFUL! DON'T DROP ME! DON'T DROP ME!
I'M TRYING!

WHOO! WE MADE IT! I JUST NEED TO PUT YOU DOWN FOR A...
NO!

PLEASE! I CAN'T STAND TO BE IN THIS BUILDING ANY LONGER!
THERE'S A BACK DOOR RIGHT BEHIND US. OUTSIDE, PAST THE GATE, THERE'S A BENCH. JUST GET ME THAT FAR. WE CAN REST THERE.

SO WITH THE VERY LAST OUNCE OF MY STRENGTH, I GOT HIM TO THAT BENCH.
THANK YOU. YOU HAVE NO IDEA WHAT YOU HAVE DONE FOR ME.
YOU'RE WELCOME.

I JUST... HAHH...?

YOU'RE STANDING.

THEN HE SHED A SINGLE TEAR AS HE SAID TO ME...
MY DEAR MARA, YOU'RE ALMOST TOO SWEET TO KILL.
HE SHED A TEAR FOR YOU?

HE SAID, "MY PEOPLE CALL IT A CROCODILE TEAR. SOME OF THEM SAY IT IS THE LAST MORSEL OF REMORSE IN OUR HUMAN SHELL. OTHERS THINK IT IS DUE TO A CHEMICAL SHIFT CAUSED BY THE TRANSFORMATION. I THINK IT'S JUST BECAUSE THE TRANSFORMATION STINGS A BIT."
TRANSFORMATION? INTO WHAT?

A VAMPIRE.

SO NATURALLY, I MADE A BREAK FOR IT.
WAIT A MINUTE...
...THIS STORY DOESN'T MAKE SENSE. WHY WOULD A VAMPIRE NEED YOU TO CARRY HIM DOWN A FLIGHT OF STAIRS?
HE CAN'T SET FOOT ON HOLLOWED GROUND. IT'S JUST AS HARMFUL AS HOLY WATER. HE NEEDED ME TO CARRY HIM OVER IT. TWO PRIESTS TRAPPED HIM IN THAT TOWER OVER A CENTURY AGO. THEY BELIEVED THAT KILLING WAS WRONG, EVEN IF IT WAS A VAMPIRE. SO THEY LOCKED HIM WHERE HE COULDN'T HURT ANYONE.

HE'S A VAMPIRE, WHY DIDN'T HE JUST FLY OUT?
IN THE REAL WORLD, ONLY VAMPIRES WITH WINGS CAN FLY.
NOW WHERE WAS I?

I TRIED TO RUN, BUT HE WAS SO FAST! IT WAS LIKE HE JUST APPEARED BEHIND ME!

I WAS CERTAIN HE'D KILL ME.

HOW DID YOU GET AWAY?

WELL?
WHY ARE YOU CRYING?
IT'S THE LAST MORSEL OF REMORSE ESCAPING MY MORTAL SHELL.

AAAAAAHH!
HLLKK!
WHY MARA? WHY? I THOUGHT WE HAD SOMETHING SPECIAL?
AN HOUR AGO, THERE WAS NO PERSON IN THE WORLD THAT I CARED FOR MORE.
BUT DON'T WORRY, YOU'RE ABOUT TO BECOME SOMETHING EVEN MORE SPECIAL. YOU'RE GOING TO BE THE FIRST HUMAN I EVER TASTE.

NOOOOAAA!!
THE END

1920s...
From the journals of Aloysius Claxton, Monster Hunter Extraordinaire... this is the true tale of the Claxton family. I begin this tale near my... end.
When I was a much younger man, our family home was taken over by bloodsucking monsters. By creatures of the night who wanted to take my family's fortune for their own.
They wanted us dead.
So it was up to me as their son... as the man of the house...
Nothing would stop me.

1930s...
No place would stop me. No matter where they went, there I was.
No matter who they were...
STAND STRAIGHT AND FACE ME, DEMON. I WILL...
FOLLOWED ME FROM THE LANDS, HAVE YOU? WHY CLAXTON? WHATSOEVER POSSESSED YOU TO COME HERE?
I WILL DEPOSE YOU. I WILL DESTROY YOU.
HA! I LAUGH AT YOUR NONSENSE, CLAXTON. YOU ARE NOTHING BUT A GNAT.
STEP FORWARD, BEAST, AND ACCEPT YOUR FATE.

1940s...
They took me everywhere around the world, these bastards did.
They put me in dire situations constantly. In wars aplenty.
It made me fear for my life more than any bombs or dictators ever could.
YOU THERE! STAND AND FACE ME!
I have seen things I will never forget.

1950s...
FIRST NATIONAL B
And I've been witness to many odd things.
Some very bizarre things.

1960s...
Getting to teach my daughter the trade... getting to teach her my tips and tricks...
Nothing more I ever wanted.
DAD!
I'M COMING. JUST HOLD ON AND DON'T GET BIT.
SORRY TO SPOOK YOU, ELVIE. I'M GLAD YOU HAD MY BACK THOUGH.
ANYTIME DAD. WHAT'S NEXT?
LET'S LISTEN TO SOME OF THIS MUSIC.

1970s....
But time is unkind. It catches up to you no matter what you want to happen. It leaves you behind while others must take your place.
BSIDINE & AMSON EXPORTS

THIS IS YOUR JOURNAL NOW. TAKE CARE OF IT. USE IT. LEARN FROM IT.
YOU'VE SHOWN IT TO ME BEFORE BUT YOU'VE NEVER REALLY EXPLAINED IT.
IT'S MY LIFE'S STORY. IT HOLDS EVERYTHING I'VE DONE, EVERYTHING I'VE ACCOMPLISHED, AND ALL OF MY GREATEST GLORIES AND TRIUMPHS.
IS THAT IT?
THERE ARE MANY TRAGEDIES AND FAILINGS AS WELL. I SPEAK OF YOUR MOTHER IN THERE.
I NEVER KNEW HER.
SHE WAS MY GREATEST TREASURE BEFORE YOU. I WOULD HAVE GIVEN THIS ALL UP FOR HER IF SHE'D ASKED.
SHE DIDN'T?
SHE DIDN'T HAVE THE CHANCE. SHE WAS TAKEN FROM ME BY ONE OF... THEM. I HOPE TO SEE HER AGAIN, IF THERE IS SOMETHING AFTER.
I HOPE THERE IS.
ME TOO.
NOW GO. FIGHT THE GOOD FIGHT AND KEEP THE FAMILY NAME GOING. I'M GOING TO SLEEP NOW.
I LOVE YOU DAD.
GOODBYE, MY DAUGHTER. AND GODSPEED.

LEAVE US ALONE. WE'RE NOT DOING ANYTHING WRONG.
THE PIER IS OFF LIMITS. YOU SUCKERS HAVE BEEN TALKING FOR TOO LONG.
WE OWN THE PIER. WHO DO YOU THINK YOU ARE?
ME?
I'M ELVIE CLAXTON. AND YOU'RE ALL GOING TO DIE.

The story lives on and thrives with me now. And will thrive forever as long as the Claxton name survives. I will not falter. I will not fail. We are the Hunters and we will destroy them all.

CLAXTON & CLAXTON VS.

STORY: CW COOKE
ART: KURT BELCHER
LETTERS: MICAH MYERS

EMERIK
TANK!
WRITTEN BY MICHAEL NORWITZ

PH'NGLUI
MGLW'NAFH
C'THULU
R'LYEH
WGAH'NAGL
FHTAGN!!!
ILLUSTRATED BY
PHILLIP JOHNSON

SPLUH-
PLUNK
SKLUNCH
SKLUNCH
SEVEN TEARS
BY
ROB HEBERT
COME ON,
COME ON,
FISHY...
A MERMAID?

EH?!
YIPE!
WAIT! DON'T GO!
WHAT ARE YOU DOING OUT HERE?
I LIVE OUT HERE.
BY YOURSELF?
I DO EVERYTHING BY MYSELF.

WHAT ABOUT YOUR FRIENDS?
I DON'T HAVE ANY FRIENDS.
ME EITHER...
WE SHOULD BE FRIENDS!
YOU COULD LIVE WITH ME.
LIVE LIKE ME.

BUT I CAN'T EVEN SWIM.
I CAN SHOW YOU HOW.
WHAT IF I WANT TO GO BACK?
YOU WON'T.
NOT AFTER YOU GET USED TO THE WATER.
ALL YOU HAVE TO DO IS TAKE THE FIRST STEP...
...end

<h1 style="text-align:center"><u>The Calladseelee</u></h1>

Written By Jack Holder, Illustrated by Saint Yak

"Lock up your daughters, your sons, and yourself besides. The Calladseelee hunts tonight."

The Calladseelee. The storyteller paused. He reveled in the tale, the reaction that befell even a crowded tavern. Grown men would look up from their cups, stare for a time in his direction, before hurriedly returning to their drinks. But they listened, he knew they listened.

"The moon is high, and tinged with blood. One of the favorite times for the beast. He likes the light, adores the silver and crimson. It reminds him of his claws, how the creature wants his claws to match the colors.

"Do you know of the Calladseelee?" There were new people in town tonight. Three in particular, gathered close to the storyteller by the fireplace. Two women, one man. They leaned closer, and stared at him, which was unusual. Too oft he had to scheme and outright lie for his supper. Perhaps tonight he would be fed.

"The Calladseelee is a monster, a legend to our fair town." He drew himself up to his full height. A quick adjustment and his shadow grew to disappear into the rafters. He hooked his fingers into claws, and swept forward in his best grimace. "He slithers out of the shadows, and snatches

up any too careless to run across his path. Good, maligned, young or old, none are safe once his sights are set on their flesh.”

One of the woman, a pretty young thing in a sturdy brown tunic and pants, huddled into her chair. She fingered the bow at her side for comfort. The man, a specimen of fine physique, snorted. He engulfed his chair, and carried a short sword at his hip. The storyteller could well imagine that the man knew how to use it.

The third was squirrelled away in a black cloak. Definitely a she, given the face that had appeared before the drinks had arrived, she was a slight thing. The cloak, which would be roomy on her male companion, almost seemed formless and without a girl hidden in its folds.

The storyteller swept forward. “There is no escape, my dear,” he whispered. “The Calladseelee finds all.”

A dagger flashed out of the folds. Made of black metal, it glinted in the firelight as it rested an inch from the storyteller’s throat. He grimaced, his hands held up in peace rather than horror.

“Grace,” the man muttered. “Put it away. We’re here to talk.”

The storyteller frowned. Talk? The seated man motioned for him to rest in an opened chair. And no one but the three newcomers were truly listening to him. He sat.

“I’m Pius,” the man grunted more than spoke. He would not look the other man in the eye, content to stare into the fire. “The two women are Gloraea and Gratia. We heard you talking about the Calladseelee.”

All heard him talking about the beast. But rather than speak the words, he nodded. Pius and Gloraea smiled.

“What do you know of the beast?”

“All too much,” he hung his head. “For a legend of darkness, the Calladseelee leaves much of its work around the town.”

“We have heard,” Gloraea murmured. “It’s attracting attention. And we would like to help this town, if we can.”

“Yes,” Pius smiled. “Ridding the world of the beast is a challenge.”

Rid the world of the Calladseelee? Was that even possible? It had wrought such fury, there did not seem to be a time when the monster did not stalk the night. The mere thought of killing it could not even enter the mind.

But the three seemed determined. Perhaps they could meet the terror.

“How do we find the creature?” Gloraea asked.

“No one has seen the Calladseelee,” the storyteller said.

“But there must be rumors,” Gratia finally peeked her head out of the robe. “A lair, a hiding place, someplace for an ambush.”

“A lair?”

“Yes, there must be some rumor,” Pius pressed.

“There is no rumor about the Calladseelee’s lair.” The storyteller pointed out the door. “Its house is on Carrion Road.”

Everyone knew about the lair. The town had learned to not stray near Carrion Road. The beast may kill with impunity, but he took pleasure in his own street. No one had glimpsed his house in five years. It was safer that way.

"Take us there." Pius stood up, as did the women. They laid money on the table, and made towards the door.

Take them there? Take them to the Calladseelee? To do so was insanity, especially for one who knew even half the tales that went through the storyteller's head.

His stomach rumbled, reminding him that he never got paid for his tale.

"Will you provide dinner?" he asked.

Pius slapped at his belt. The money pouch jingled, crisp and clear.

"And more besides," the man promised.

The night air was warm, muggy. The summer had been especially hot, and even long after sunset the air hung about them, cloying. Soon Gloraea had removed her vest, and Pius had loosened his collared shirt. Gratia remained in her cloak, and huddled into it closer as they neared Carrion Road.

The storyteller felt fine. Even in this heat, he had felt most comfortable by the fire. He was always on the slim side, and had developed a knack for running at the earliest sign of trouble. It made life so much easier.

Talking did that as well. And talk he did, all the way through. He asked questions, to be sure, but the three ignored him whenever possible. This was not a night to enjoy, it was work.

Well, one ignored him. Pius had heard all he had ever cared to about the Calladseelee. This was a monster, and a fierce one to be sure, but it was nothing worse than what he had seen before. He had been tracking anything like this legend, and hoped that it would finally bring him some interest.

There weren't too many people like Pius in the world. He did not want to rid the beast as one of the problems plaguing the land. The land held very little interest for him, problems even less. Pius had grown up away from such petty, small things such as problems. Those were for lesser folk.

No, the Calladseelee called to him as a challenge. Finally something worthy of his considerable talents. He would rid the world of this creature. It would remain on his wall for all time.

They turned towards Carrion Road. Gloraea could see the buildings changing before her. This had never been a prosperous town, but it was all too clear that the closer one got to the Calladseelee, the worse it got. At this time of night there should be lights up, minor spells to help light the way. Even in this heat, Gloraea wanted to light a torch just so she could see where she was going.

This was unacceptable. The beast had to be rid of this land, this life. The woman listened closer as the storyteller rambled on. But for all these kills, there was no mention of weaknesses. He killed only at night, and there was no never about the beast. Solitary women, groups of drunkards, patrol guards, at any time of darkness. Throats ripped out, chunks of flesh missing, whole body parts rent to pieces. The only thing that determined a Calladseelee kill was his laughter cutting into the world.

Gratia knew about killing. She had killed…thirty-three monsters to date. This one might be tougher, but there hadn't been a living creature that could stand up to little Mercy. She touched the handle, knew that it recognized her thoughts. Little Mercy always knew when the girl was thinking about it.

It wasn't her fault. She had been hungry, and the Duchess had whole rooms just devoted to food. While her people starved she feasted like some fat boar that couldn't even be bothered to move off her rump. Even collected treasures, maybe something Gratia could have sold when she ran off.

But that box, Little Mercy's box, had called to her. And when she picked it up, it took a piece of her soul in response. She could almost feel it in the dagger's gem. It wailed like she did, wept every day while they were apart.

The Calladseelee might be enough to appease the dagger. And if not, it might help her along the way.

The storyteller turned left, and the darkness closed in around them. There were buildings on Carrion Road, they could feel the presence of the wood frames and stone foundations. But the shadows hid all, save one.

The storyteller waved a hand towards the light. "The Calladseelee's house."

It didn't look like a lair of evil. Two stories, rickety. In need of paint. It looked like no one was going to be working on it soon either. The single light came from a windowpane on the first floor, flames flickering off the glass. Gloraea had seen many houses such as this in her travels, had slept in more than a few.

That said, she didn't want to venture any closer. The house's door was wide open, hanging on one hinge that creaked as she looked at it. The porch wasn't rotted, but promised to fall away any moment. It spoke honeyed words with its visage, but Gloraea knew better. This house was death.

The storyteller held a hand out towards the open door. "It seems you are expected, and invited in."

"So it seems," Gratia murmured. Beneath her robes she tightened her grip on Little Mercy.

"Do you accept the monster's invitation?" the storyteller asked.

"We *all* do." Pius gave a little shove. The other man stumbled over the steps, landing on his hands. "Lead the way."

He got to his feet, and thought about making a retort. Instead he walked through.

"Come on in, then."

The house was lived in. Stacks of books on the stairs, jostling the

carpet. No dust puffed up as they walked through the door. And even despite the crackling fire in the den, it seemed more pleasant in the house than outside. A host had made a concerted effort to clean up the abode.

Pius led past the main hall to the den. Dull burgundy walls, a plush chair that sat next to the stone fireplace with a corresponding footrest. A crystal glass sat next to the chair on a table, with a book open to a page.

"This is the Calladseelee's?" Pius asked. He had known lords who would have had apartments in cities arranged as such.

The elder woman shook her head. "Look closer, Pius. Something isn't right."

Up on the fireplace mantle hung a doll. It stared back at the three adventurers, questioning their presence. Why were they here? What was their purpose?

Gloraea stared at the glass, and held it up. "Still cold," She muttered. "He must have left in a hurry. Or a spell."

She hoped not. Who could tell what sort of danger they could be in if the Calladseelee could wreak magic as well?

Gratia's nose wrinkled, and frowned. "What's that smell?"

Pius snorted, and stopped. There it was, what she said. A faint smell, but present everywhere. Metallic, it didn't come from the chair or the rug. But the place was immaculate, there was not an item out of place. Nothing that could have been such a scent.

Gratia looked at the shadows, dancing on the walls. She put her hand on the frame, and shuddered.

"The walls," she whispered. "It's the walls."

Gloraea pulled out an arrow, and scraped along the structure. The paint flaked off into her outstretched hand. She took a sniff, and shuddered.

"Blood," she said. "The entire room is painted in blood."

The three checked once more that the Calladseelee was not hiding in the den before racing out. Across the hall, to the kitchen. All were armed, Pius leading the way with sword drawn. Gloraea looked behind them with an arrow resting underneath her bow. Gratia darted from one shadow to the next, Little Mercy in her hands.

The kitchen held more gore. Body parts stacked on a butcher's block, bones scattered into a refuse pile. Gloraea almost retched at a hand pointed straight at her, sitting up in a fist. The oven slid up on the opposite wall was lit and starting to heat up, the beast had to be here. But still no Calladseelee.

Instead, there was a dining table set in the middle of the kitchen. Three place settings in front of three chairs. Plates with fruit cups placed on them, utensils shining in the dim light. Crystal glasses with silk napkins placed underneath them.

The storyteller walked down the stairs. "I apologize if the fruit is not to your liking, some may be out of season."

He had changed clothes, now wearing a gray vest and loose fitting brown leggings. His chest, arms and feet were completely bare, but there was a notebook and pen in his hands. He looked at the three adventurers' expressions, and made a notation in the notebook. Confusion, almost realizing but not quite. This was amusing.

"Please, sit." he said. "You are the first three in my home…" he trailed off, and looked at the hand on the butcher's block. "Well, alive, for about seven months now."

Gloraea's bow was up in an instant. An arrow flashed forward. The storyteller snatched it out of the air, and looked at it. He tasted the tip, and nodded. "Salt and silver. Good choices."

His face stretched forward, nose elongating to a gray snout. What were once bright eyes darkened with his skin, beady and unblinking. His hair receded into a light fur, and his body stretched. Bones crackled as they extended, his arms and legs lengthening far past those of humans. The beast, for beast he must be, cracked his knuckles, and again as new ones appeared. Then his fingernails sharpened, resembling claws.

The Calladseelee loomed over the three adventurers. Pale, hairless, it was more nightmare than real. It smiled, fangs showing tips of saliva.

"Now we'll have none of that during dinner," he muttered. "Sit. Please."

Gratia was the first seated. Pius and Gloraea each followed suit. The beast set the arrow on the table, and began to set the table more.

"I must say, I do enjoy when guests are here. It is so rare, but so treasured."

He cleared the gore away from the block, and started to rummage through the cupboard. "I was going to have myself a drink, maybe a snack, but when I realized that there were three people that wanted to see me, how could I refuse?"

He frowned. "But this won't do. I am such a terrible host." The Calladseelee returned to the table, and nodded.

"It is entirely my fault. I am too used to being a bachelor, and only made enough food for one."

So he cut Gloraea's throat.

Pius and Gratia didn't even see the cut. Gloraea didn't notice until she saw her cup start to overflow. Her head rolled to one side, and toppled from her shoulders.

The Calladseelee caught her by the hair, and carried it over to the butcher's block. "I hope you like cheese," he said. "Though it may take a while to get through this rind."

Pius leaped from his chair, sword in hand. He bounded over the table, and slashed down at the Calladseelee.

The beast sidestepped the blow. The swing caught Gloraea's head, shearing it in two before burying the metal in the wood. Pius struggled for an instant, trying in vain to release the sword. Before he realized he had to let go the monster was behind him, claws around his waist.

The beast lifted the man above the butcher's block. With a heave, the Calladseelee tossed Pius to the floor. His mouth opened, dazed and confused.

The oven door flew open with a bang as it hit the bottom hinge. The Calladseelee allowed himself a smack of his lips before he threw Pius into the low fire. A scream escaped the appliance before the monster closed the door and locked it.

"Don't go anywhere," He whispered. "Now, Gratia."

Gratia had not stayed still. When the Calladseelee had turned away with the head she had run for the exit. But while the door

still hung from one hinge, she could not leave. Something barred her way, unseen. She had slashed at it with Little Mercy, and still nothing. The oven door slammed, and she ran up the stairs. Past broken bones scattered around the main hall. Towards the open door. She slammed it shut, and laid in wait.

She knew she would not have to wait long. The Calladseelee padded up the stairs, and laughed when he reached the top. "Am I going to just keep apologizing? I heartily admit it, I am alone. I am a monster, creeping through the dark."

The door snapped in two, bursting open. The Calladseelee walked in, holding an empty glass by the stem. He turned to Gratia with a sneer. "Just like you."

Gratia cut forward with Little Mercy. It caught, it tore through that wicked arm! The Calladseelee looked at his bleeding appendage in surprise.

"That hasn't happened in a while," he said.

Triumphant, Gratia struck again. She could do this!

The beast caught her by the wrist. He winced at the pressure on his bad arm. "Now, we will have no more of that." he looked at his arm, and grimaced. "That is one impressive knife."

He clamped down on her wrist, *hard*. Gratia cried out, screamed as the bones began to break. But even as her fingers weakened and loosened, Little Mercy did not fall. It did not wish to.

"Do you so wish to kill me?" the Calladseelee asked.

"I," the girl began.

"I wasn't talking to you." the Calladseelee looked at the blade. "Hmmm, a nasty piece of work. Ah, your holder. She is a pretty thing."

The two looked at the blade. The Calladseelee shook his head. "She invaded my home. You two wanted my lifeblood. That is not something I forgive slightly."

He brightened. "But there is an alternative." he raised the cup to his still-bleeding arm. He clenched again, and the cup filled. He held it out to Gratia. "Drink."

The girl almost retched. No, never. The blood wasn't red, it was black. Who knew what would happen? But Little Mercy whispered in her hand. There would be no more help from the blade.

She lifted the cup to her lips, and drank. The blood was not foul, but syrupy and sweet. She wanted to stop, but the monster held the cup tipped until its contents ran dry.

He released her, and bowed. "Thank you for a lovely dinner," he said. "But I am tired, and haven't had dinner myself. If you would take your leave, I will retire."

Gratia disappeared. Out the door, off of Carrion Road, and made her haste towards the exit of town. She wouldn't get far before the changes would start.

The Calladseelee went back to the kitchen and began to clear the table. The girl would not understand the changes, how her teeth would lengthen and recede. How they would come with warning and leave without reason. Perhaps she would embrace it, and return. But that would be months, years later. He could wait.

Gloraea was propped against the chair. She would provide food for a while, though there may be some amusement to be had for now. He did enjoy the tableau, even if it ruined his table.

The oven banged, twice. The monster groaned, and threw a fruit cup at the chair.

"Food shouldn't wriggle in the oven!" he said. "I'll get to you later."

For now, it was time to enjoy his book. It had been a good night. Company, dinner, and he might have even made himself a friend.

It was good being a monster sometimes.

THE FROZEN SCREAM
BY WALTER OSTLIE

TERROR, THY NAME IS POO

BROUGHT TO YOU BY THE BONEHEADS AT **SMACKWELL COMICS GROUP!** STORY BY **LUIS BERMUDEZ**. ART BY **ALEX BERMUDEZ**.
IN THIS INCREDIBLE ISSUE: THE ADJECTIVE-LESS **BIFF SMACKWELL!** THE UNCONTROLLABLE **KID KNUCKLES!** THE FEISTY **FREEDOM FOX!** AND **BRIGADE**, THE MULTI-MAN!

A QUARTER AND A HALF MONTHS LATER...
ALRIGHT, GUYS! THIS'LL BE A PIECE OF CAKE!
JUST MAKE SURE YOU STICK TO THE—
CHARGE!
BEST IDEA I HEARD ALL DAY, BIFF!
CAN'T SAY I DISAGREE, KNUCKLES!
FIIINE!
ARE WE JUST GONNA INTRODUCE EACH OTHER ALL DAY, OR CAN WE START BEATING UP THAT MONSTER?
I HATE TO DO THIS TO YOU BOYS, BUT IT'S THE ONLY WAY TO GET YOU ALL TO START PAYING ATTENTION.
MEAN

DON'T YOU WORRY, FOX! THIS GUY'S GONNA BE EASY! WATCH THIS!
HOWZABOUT YOU WATCH, KNUCKLES? PARTICULARLY, WATCH THE GUY THAT'S ABOUT TO—

YA-HOW-ZA!
KA-POW-ZA!
YUP.

DON'T SWEAT IT, KNUCKS! I'M LINED UP TO PUNCH HIM RIGHT UP HIS FACE!
AWESOME!
YEAH. YEAH. UP HIS FACE. HE'LL NEVER SEE THAT COMING.

LIES! HE TOTALLY SAW IT COMING!
KLONK!

YOU NERDS WITH YOUR SILLY PUNCHIES! JUST GOTTA POWER UP AND HIT IT WITH A BLAST FROM WAY BACK HERE!
RIGHT! BECAUSE A GIANT, AMORPHOUS POO MONSTER WON'T BE ABLE TO GET TO YOU FROM WAY BACK THERE.

BAKONG!
WHOA! CRAZY HEADBUTT! THAT'S NOT FAIR!
SO, YOU GUYS READY TO STICK TO THE PLAN NOW?
...MEBBE.

OKAY, BOYS! ROUND TWO!

BIFF, GET YOURSELF TOGETHER.
GET READY TO ATTACK ON MY MARK!
ROGER, WILCO!

KNUCKLES, GET YOURSELF IN POSITION TO FLANK HIM ON HIS LEFT!
YOU GOT IT!

BRIGADE, FLANK RIGHT AND MAKE A DUPLICATE THAT CAN DO SOMETHING USEFUL FOR ONCE!
YA KNOW, YOU'RE GONNA JINX MY DUPES, YOU KEEP TALKING LIKE THAT.

BWOOP!
SUP DUDE! WHAT CAN YOU DO?
I DUNNO, BUT I BET IT'S COOL. HERE GOES NOTHIN'!

eh... CATS!
SPARKLY CATS!
BRIGADE! WHAT ARE WE SUPPOSED TO DO WITH A BUNCH OF CATS?!
UGH!

DON'T WORRY, BRIGS, I GOT 'IM!
KNUCKLES, WAIT!

TRUST ME, FOX! I GOT THIS! JUST ONE UPPER--
WHAT THE--?!

RUN LIKE SISSIES! HE HEALS HIS WOUNDS WITH POO!

POOOO!!!

OH, CRAP! IT SMELLS LIKE GARY, INDIANA!

WELL, THAT WAS A QUICK EXIT. HE'S GONE.
SEE? YOU JINXED ME.
MAYBE IF WE JUST PUNCH HIM HARDER...
THAT'S NOT GONNA WORK. WE'LL NEED TO PUNCH HIM EVEN HARDER THAN THAT.
MEAN GREEN LATRINE
OH, BOYS...
I THINK WE'RE GONNA NEED A LITTLE HELP HERE.
COPY THAT, BUT WHO CAN HELP US UNDO THIS EMERGENCY QUICKLY?

HALF A DAY AND A HALF LATER, AT Q.U.E* HQ...
*QUICK UNDOERS OF EMERGENCIES

ALRIGHT, TEAM, HERE'S WHAT WE KNOW.
ALL ATTEMPTS TO STOP OR EVEN SLOW THIS MONSTER'S RAMPAGE HAVE TOTALLY FAILED.
WE CAN'T FIGHT IT OR REASON WITH IT.
SO WHAT CAN WE DO?
WE'VE ENGINEERED A DEVICE THAT SHOULD BE ABLE TO CONTAIN THE MONSTER.
ONCE YOU CONTAIN IT, YOU WILL CONTACT US AND WE'LL PICK IT UP IN ONE OF OUR SPACE CRAFT.
WE'LL DELIVER THE THING STRAIGHT INTO THE SUN, IF WE HAVE TO!
ARE YOU SURE WE CAN'T JUST PUNCH IT MORE?
YOU CAN'T SOLVE ALL YOUR PROBLEMS WITH YOUR FISTS, KNUCKLES.
NOW, HOW DO WE FIND THE DAMN THING, DIRECTOR CRISTIANA PENTECOSTES FUENTE DE VIDA?

PLEASE, JUST CALL ME CRISTIANA. WE'RE PRESSED FOR TIME.
THIS MAP SHOWS ALL THE SPOTS AROUND SUPER CITY THAT IT'S HIT.
WE CAN'T FIGURE OUT ITS PATTERN OF ATTACK, OR HOW A CREATURE THIS LARGE IS EVEN MOVING AROUND THE CITY UNNOTICED!
IT'S HIT SOME CONSTRUCTION SITES, SOME MUSIC FESTIVALS, EVEN W.H.E.N. HQ!

W.H.E.N.
OH, HEY, REMEMBER THIS PLACE?
HA! OH YEAH! THE GUY WOULDN'T ADMIT HIS TIME MACHINE WAS A PORTAPOTTY!

WAIT, THAT'S IT!
I KNEW IT! WHAT'S IT?
IT'S THE PORTAPOTTIES! THEY'RE AT ALL THE SITES IT'S ATTACKED!
I SEE! HE'S USING THEM LIKE TELEPORTAPOTTIES!
EXACTLY!

FOX, YOU'RE A GENIUS!
THAT'S WHY SHE GETS PAID THE BIG BUCKS!

SHE GETS PAID?!

LATER THAT NIGHT, AT A CONSTRUCTION SITE INSIDE THE BURRITO-MAX NUCLEAR POWER PLANT INDUSTRIAL ZONE -- THE LAST KNOWN PLACE IN THE AREA WITH PORTAPOTTIES THAT HAVE NOT YET BEEN SULLIED BY THE MONSTER...
NO SIGN OF IT YET.
IT'S NOT UNDER THIS CEMENT TRUCK.
AHOY! I SPY YONDER TWENTYFOLD PORTABLE CRAPPERIES! LET US AWAY!
GOOD JOB, KNUCKLES! QUICK, LET'S SPLIT UP AND SEARCH THEM ALL!
BWOOP!
BWOOP!
BWOOP!
ON IT!

MOMENTS LATER, AFTER ALL THE OTHER PORTAPOTTIES HAVE BEEN SEARCHED...
THIS IS THE LAST ONE.
OPEN IT, BIFF.
WHY DO I GOTTA--?
BECAUSE YOUR RIDICULOUSLY HUGE MUSCLES LOOK LIKE THEY WANT TO.
LADY, YOU ARE NOT WRONG.

SCHLEMIEL!
NOPE, NOT HERE. DOESN'T EVEN SMELL LIKE POO.

POO?
YES, BRIGADE. THE THING IS MADE OF POO.
HUH? I DIDN'T--

AAAAHHHHHHHH!!!
POO!!!

BIFF, USE THE THING ON IT!
YOU SAY THAT LIKE I HAVEN'T BEEN ITCHING TO FIRE THIS BIG-ASS CANNON ALL DAY!
BRIGADE, POWER CHECK, IN CASE THIS THING DOESN'T WORK!
SOUND OFF, GUYS! POWERS?
UHH...
I GOT LIKE, THESE WATERY POWERS.
I'M FRIGGIN' HUUUGE!
YOU REALLY THINK IT WON'T WORK?!
IT SURELY WILL, KNUCKLES, BUT IT NEVER HURTS TO BE PREPARED FOR THE UNEXPECTED!
POO!!!

HA! GOT IT!
SKLOUNS!

WHOA! IT'S MELTING THE POO GUY?
I DON'T THINK IT'S SUPPOSED TO DO THAT...

OH, GROSS! IT WENT ALL DIARRHEA INTO THAT HOLE FULL OF TOXIC SLIME!

HEY! MAYBE IT KILLED ITSELF! JOB WELL DONE, FRIENDS!
HUH... MAYBE?
MAYBE, BUT WE HAVE TO CHECK. WE CAN'T JUST ASSUME IT'S DEAD.
YOU KNOW WHAT THEY SAY: "DON'T CALL 'EM CHICKENS BEFORE THEY HATCH!"

NOBODY EVER SAID THAT.

Freedom Fox!

I'M ALRIGHT, KNUCKLES! BUT I DON'T KNOW FOR HOW LONG!
ALRIGHT, SIT TIGHT! I'LL HAVE YOU OUT OF THERE IN A JIF!
MMM. PEANUT BUTTER!
GIGAPOO!!!
KNUCKS, STAY FOCUSED! YOU'RE DISTRACTING YOURSELF AGAIN!
RIGHT, BIFF!
I THINK MY STRETCHY POWER'S BROKE!
I THINK MY WATER'S BROKE!
BRIGADE, DO SOMETHING ABOUT YOUR DUPES!

IT'S TOO STRONG! I CAN'T GET FREE!
AND FOR THE FIRST TIME IN MY LIFE, PUNCHING ISN'T FIXING ANYTHING AT ALL!

YEAH I'M NOT GETTING ANYWHERE HERE, EITHER!

MY BLASTS STILL DON'T DO JACK TO THIS THING!
UMM... MY WATER POWERS ARE KINDA UNDER CONTROL!
UH, MY SITUATION STILL KINDA SUCKS!

I'M FRIGGIN' HUUUGE!
THANKS FOR THE SAVE, BRIGADE!
BIFF, GRAB THAT CEMENT TRUCK AND CHUCK IT AT THE MONSTER!

ROGER THAT, CAP'N!

RIGHT ON TARGET!
PLOINCH!

BRIGADES, BLOW UP THE TRUCK AND DOUSE THE CEMENT!
WAY AHEAD OF YA, FOX!
ZEEP!

K-KRAK
K-KRAK
THE GIANT POO MONSTER TRIES TO SHAKE OFF THE EFFECTS OF THE QUICK-DRYING CEMENT THAT HAS MIXED WITH HIS AMORPHOUS BODY, BUT HARDO BRAND CEMENT DON'T MESS AROUND! THE MONSTER IS STOPPED DEAD IN ITS TRACKS!

WE DID IT! HE'S ALL PETRIFIED UP LIKE SOME KIND OF MONOLITHIC POO MAN!
LIKE A CACA-LOSSUS OF RHODES!
UH, GROSS?

MEGAGIGAPOO!!!

WHAT THE SHIT?!
LANGUAGE!
HOW THE CRAP ARE WE GONNA BEAT THIS THING NOW? WE COULDN'T DO IT BEFORE, AND NOW HE'S GONE ALL BATTLE-ARMORED BOWEL MOVEMENT!
ACTUALLY, THIS MIGHT BE OUR CHANCE TO FINALLY GET RID OF HIM, FOR GOOD!
HOW DO YOU FIGURE?
HE'S SOLID NOW! YOU KNOW WHAT THAT MEANS!
OH YEAH...

YOU GOTTA PUNCH IT!!!

POO?!

CRAPLOWZA!

HMM! THAT WAS KINDA EASY, ONCE WE STARTED WORKING TOGETHER!
LOOKS LIKE THE REAL MONSTER HERE WAS OUR LACK OF TEAMWORK!
Y'KNOW, THAT'S THE CUTEST BIT OF CHARACTER DEVELOPMENT I'VE EVER SEEN!

CUTE, YES! BUT LITTLE KNUCKLES IS FORGETTING SOMETHING! HIS MOTHER FORBADE HIM FROM DEVELOPING CHARACTER IN CUTE WAYS UNLESS SHE'S THERE TO SEE IT!
WUTDAHUH?!

OH, NO! MY MOTHER'S GONNA KILL ME!!!

Today
A
Thursday
Wednesday
Everything I touch
The Devil turns
to Gold
I made a Deal with
the Devil
and do not
remember
What for
The Deal
Adapted for Comics from an original story
By Daniel Sharner
by Zac Skellington Conley
about 6 months ago
average life
Tortured struggling writer
No love life
average job
Wounded Fish
Advertising Agency
Average boss
Father Figure
I didn't like my life
Gentle Soul

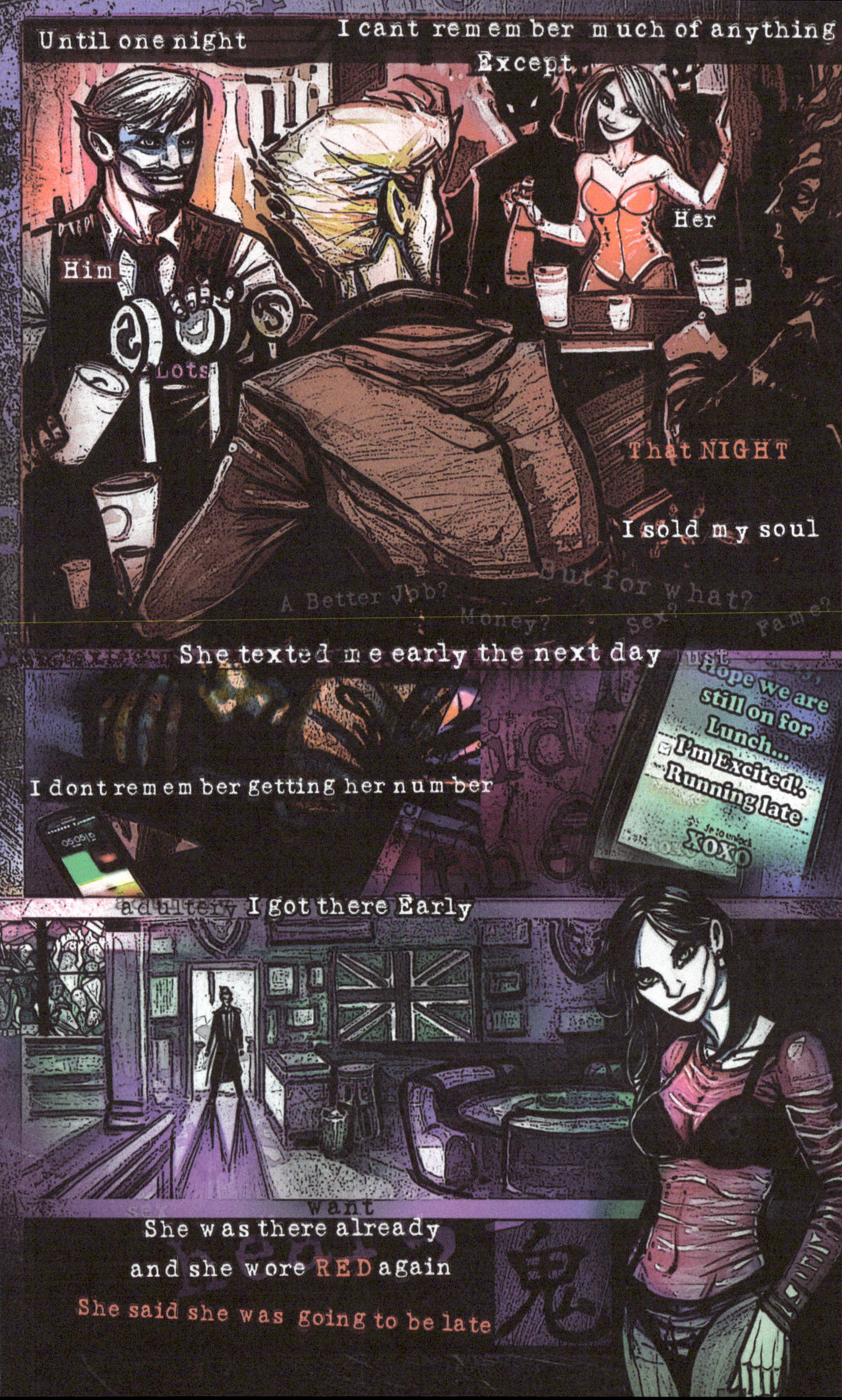

Until one night
I cant remember much of anything
Except...
Him
Lots
Her
That NIGHT
I sold my soul
But for what?
A Better Job?
Money?
Sex?
Fame?
She texted me early the next day
Hope we are still on for Lunch... I'm Excited! Running late
XOXO
I dont remember getting her number
I got there Early
She was there already
and she wore RED again
She said she was going to be late

isn't that the bartender from last night.
He said our Bill was on the house

He said
Everything
will be on the house
until
I get what I asked for

and
then
I
will
die

odd
thing
to say

One of the best nights of my life
Him
I Became the Devil's toy... right here
Met Natasha's friends
Got to hang out with the band
Him
Us
The Band even offered me a job,
...go on tour and write about their travels
I said no

Natasha Just Disappeared
I am in no way the worlds smartest anything
DAILY TELEGRAPH
Local Man wins World's Smartest Gameshow
ARROGANCE
Me
Me
DAILY TELEGRAPH
EST. 1876
Smartest Person Finds Ancient Diamond
$1,000,000
The World's SMARTEST
PERSON
Me
DAILY TELEGRAPH
EST. 1876
World's smartest person Saves Family From
I started to win at everything
and it terrified me
I tried to run away in fear
but found only greater prosperity...
everything prosperous brought me
only
even greater
fear
Local Band Killed in Tragic Bus Accident
GUAR
It's terrifying to think THE DEVIL could come
collecting at any moment with every new
fortune that crossed my path

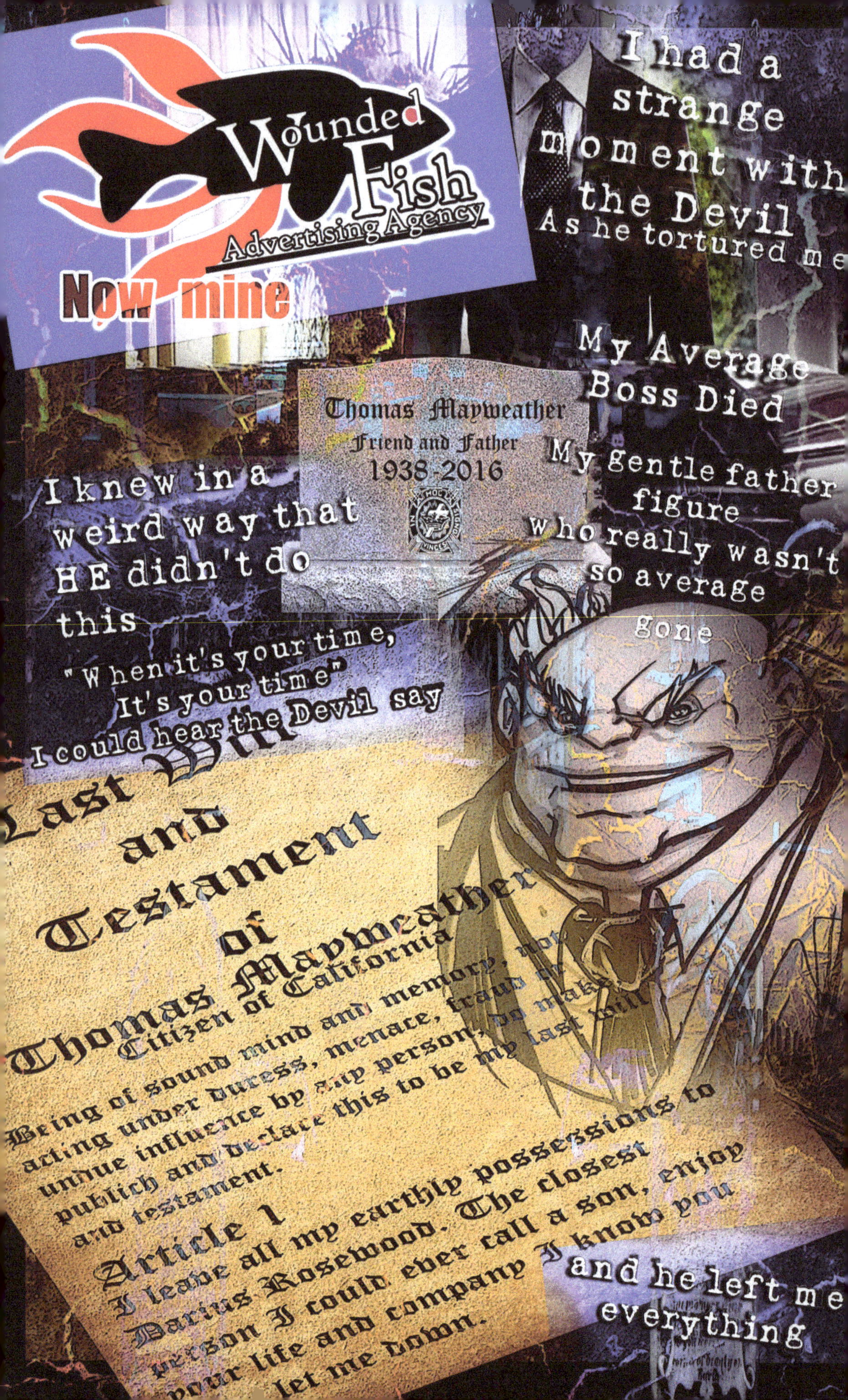

Wounded Fish
Advertising Agency
Now mine
I had a strange moment with the Devil
As he tortured me
My Average Boss Died
My gentle father figure
who really wasn't so average
gone
Thomas Mayweather
Friend and Father
1938-2016
I knew in a weird way that HE didn't do this
"When it's your time, It's your time"
I could hear the Devil say
Last Will and Testament of Thomas Mayweather
Citizen of California
Being of sound mind and memory, not acting under duress, menace, fraud or undue influence by any person, do make, publish and declare this to be my last will and testament.
Article 1
I leave all my earthly possessions to Darius Rosewood. The closest person I could ever call a son, enjoy your life and company I know you let me down.
and he left me everything

Some say you dance with the devil
the DEVIL doesn't change, he changes you.
He dances with you

One decision after another and still no closer
No closer to any answer and now....now
I am starting to see ...
things.

Dark things that lurk in the world of man.
What do these things matter if I end up alone

and

I already know my fate?

Even when I do things for all the right reasons
I feel like I make matters only worse. I'm so
scared of even my own shadow of what might
be hiding inside it.

The greatest trick the Devil ever played is convincing the world he doesn't exist.
and I was one of them.
I still don't know if I believe
I would like to think I still have some choices
But none of us do.
I'm one step closer to the end and I just don't know
how to do the next...anything
A life and things people would find endless joy and
happiness in are my torment,
I can't out run HIM.
Is today the day?
my final day
I'm so consumed...
I can't even find comfort in the life I have now
Natasha
Her
what was the Deal?

ONLINE PREDATOR
Art by @Lady Beaver
words by @SteveWaldinger
Thanks to the internet, I can set up a DINNER DATE without having to leave the HOUSE!
What do you say we SPICE things up a little?
I guess that'd be okay, as long as I'm home by nine.
Why are there always APPLES in my mouth when I need to say a SAFEWORD?
Mustard sure does make a sweater taste great! I'd save you some leftovers, but, well, YOU'RE THE MEAL!
MMM, head sticks are my favorite!
I wonder if OK CUPID knows they make a great ALL YOU CAN EAT BUFFET?
ok cupid
I'm glad I finally made the decision to try ONLINE DATING! Hope she likes flowers!
knock knock
Yay, flowers! They make the perfect SALAD!

THE PROMISE

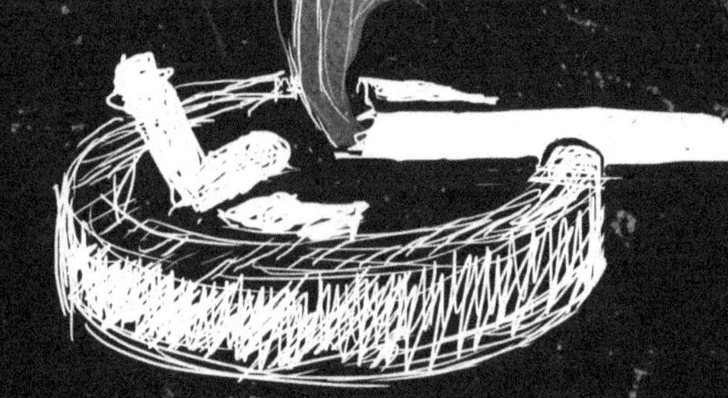

STORY FELIX YIN
ART & LETTERING ALEX BODNAR
EDITING RUSSELL NOHELTY

MOMMY
HMM

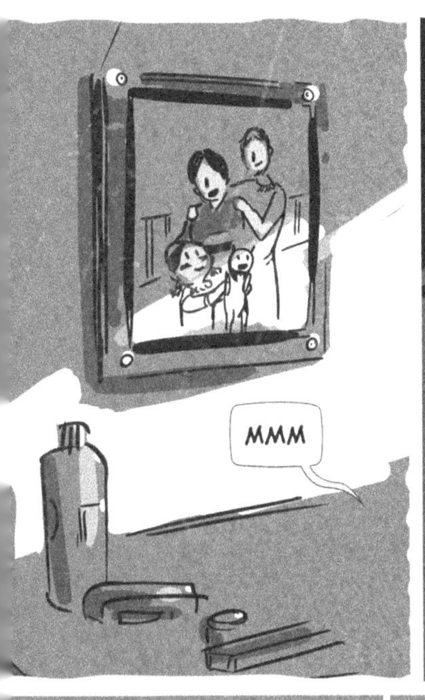

MMM

MMM

CHARGING...

CLICK
CLICK

TOSS

TIK
TIK
TIK
SIGH

Tom,
I went to Earl's
to get on a quick
errand. My phone's
charging, but I'll
be right back.

Love, Tanya

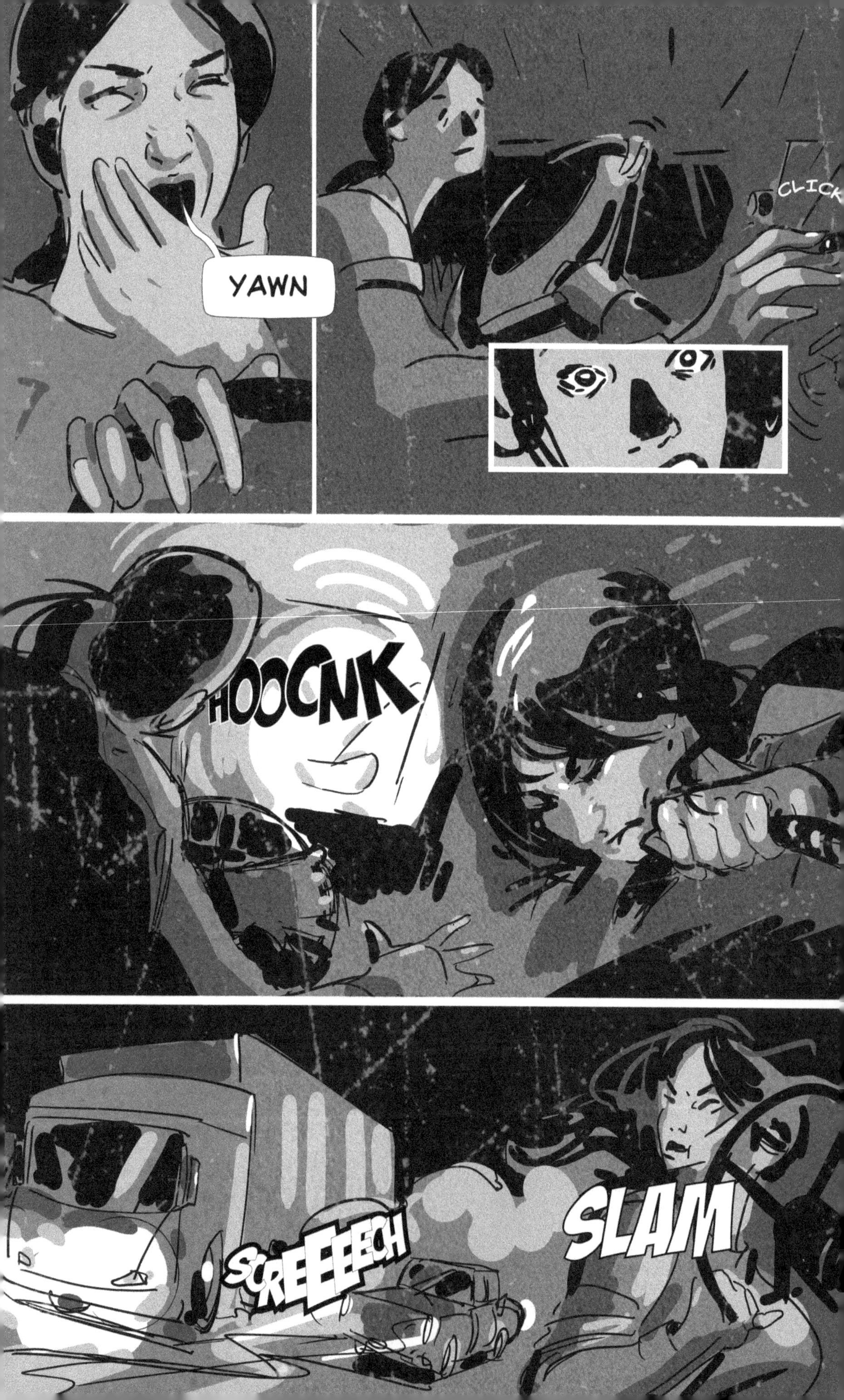

YAWN
CLICK

HOOCNK

SCREEEECH
SLAM

CLICK

OOOOF

HUFF

EARL'S
MINI MART
BEST IN-HOUSE
JERKY
2 miles
OPEN
24
HOUR
I BET IF I CUT THROUGH THE CORNFIELD, I CAN SHAVE OFF A MILE.

HEY...

?
WHERE ARE YOU GOING?

PSST!
HEY!
OVER HERE!
WHY ARE YOU RUNNING?
WHO IS THAT?
THUD

OMFF!
STAB

GREAT! FIRST THE TRUCK AND NOW THIS!

HE BETTER HAVE THOSE FRENCH IMPORTS I LIKE!
LAND

WHERE ARE YOU GOING?

TANYA?

HEY EARL!
BOY AM I GLAD TO SEE YOU!
ARE YOU OKAY?
I DON'T THINK SO...

I'VE BEEN...
HEARING THINGS.

IT'S PROBABLY A CONCUSSION OR SOMETHING.

DO YOU THINK I CAN USE YOUR PHONE?
I TOTALED TOM'S TRUCK.

YEAH! OF COURSE!
BY THE WAY...

DO YOU WANT TO TRY MY NEWEST JERKY? I THINK IT'S MY BEST RECIPE YET!

NO THANKS, EARL. I'M NOT THE JERKY TYPE. I WAS KIND OF HOPING TO GET SOME CIGARETTES.

YOU SURE, TANYA? YOU'RE ALREADY SHAKY. SOME JERKY COULD BE EXACTLY WHAT YOU NEED.
BESIDES, YOU TOLD ME TO NEVER...

SCOOT

THANKS, EARL. BUT, I THINK I'M JUST ON EDGE

DON'T WORRY YOURSELF OVER THAT TRUCK! I CAN FIX IT GOOD AS NEW!

THANKS, EARL. I NEED A MOMENT TO CLEAR MY HEAD OUTSIDE.

MOMMY
BABY?

IT CAN'T BE.

WHAT'S THAT IN YOUR HAND, MOMMY?

YOU LIED.
YOU LIED ABOUT WHAT HAPPENED WITH OUR BARN.
YOU PROMISED DADDY YOU WOULD STOP.
YOU LIED TO HIM, TOO.
NO...

MAXI DIED
IN OUR BARN
YOU EVEN MADE UP A STORY
TO THE POLICE TO COVER
UP WHAT ACTUALLY
HAPPENED TO ME!

WHAT THE...?

DO MY BIDDING!
STORY & ART BY BOBBY TIMONY

PARDON ME, M'LADY! HOW WOULD YOU LIKE TO MAKE A BIT OF COIN AS MY LAB ASSISTANT?
WE SHALL PLAY GODS AND MAKE FOR OURSELVES A MONSTER! WHAT SAY YOU?

NAH.

NO, SHE SAYS! WHO DOES SHE THINK SHE IS? MY MOTHER? EVERYBODY ALWAYS REJECTS ME! AND I'M SUCH A NICE GUY!!
NO ONE CAN RECOGNIZE MY TRUE GENIUS! THEY ARE ALL IMBECILES, THE LOT OF THEM!
REJECT ME, WILL THEY? WELL, NO LONGER! SOON THEY'LL SEE! THEY'LL ALL SEE...
FEET

MY PARENTS!
PRETTY GIRLS
WHO SMELL NICE!
THE POLICE!
STRAY CATS!
THE MANAGER AT THE
SHOPWELL!
OLD MAN WILSON!
STEVE!
THEY'LL ALL PAY FOR
SAYING NO TO ME!!

AT LAST!
IT'S ALIVE!!
GO, MY
BEAUTIFUL
CREATION!
DESTROY MY
ENEMIES!
DO MY BIDDING!

NAH.
THE END!

THE MIRROR
YARD SALE
WRITTEN BY: GREG SMITH
ILLUSTRATED BY: MEESCHA DARE

YARD
SALE
APPLES

How much is
this mirror?

It's free if
you can take it.

Thank you
ma'am!

Bye now.....

Arriving home...
KLUNK

TAP
TAP
TAP

I'll call you later, now get out of here!

TAP
TAP

TAP
TAP
TAP

NOOOOO!!!!!!!!!!!
GASP!!

What a strange dream...

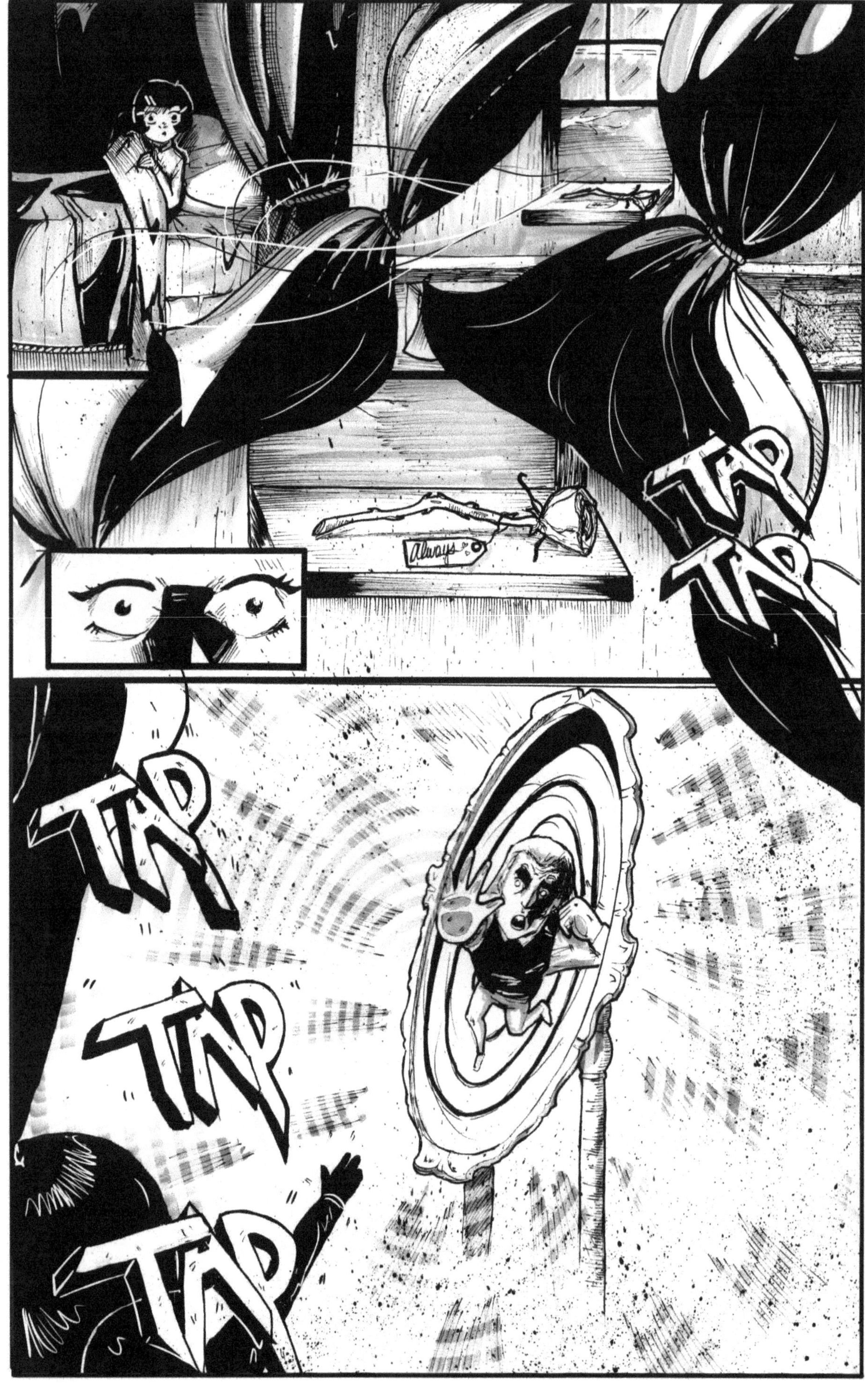

always
TAP
TAP
TAP
TAP
TAP

SHE'D ALREADY RISEN AND SET 270 BILLION TIMES BEFORE THE FIRST ORGANIC WIGGLE MADE ITS RIPPLE IN THE SEA.

BUT UNTIL THAT DAY, NEVER HAD A SECOND STAR BURNED OVER THE WORLD'S HORIZON...

...A WORLD DOOMED TO END BEFORE IT HAD THE CHANCE TO BEGIN.

WE WERE CALLED ENLLI. SMALL GODS DWELLING INSIDE THE BOWELS OF A GREAT COSMIC GOD...
...INHABITING A POCKET OF HIS ALMIGHTY DIGESTION.
WE WERE SLAVES, AND KNEW NOT YET OUR POTENTIAL FOR POWER...
BELLY OF THE BEAST
JOSH WAGNER
FREEDOM DRUDGE

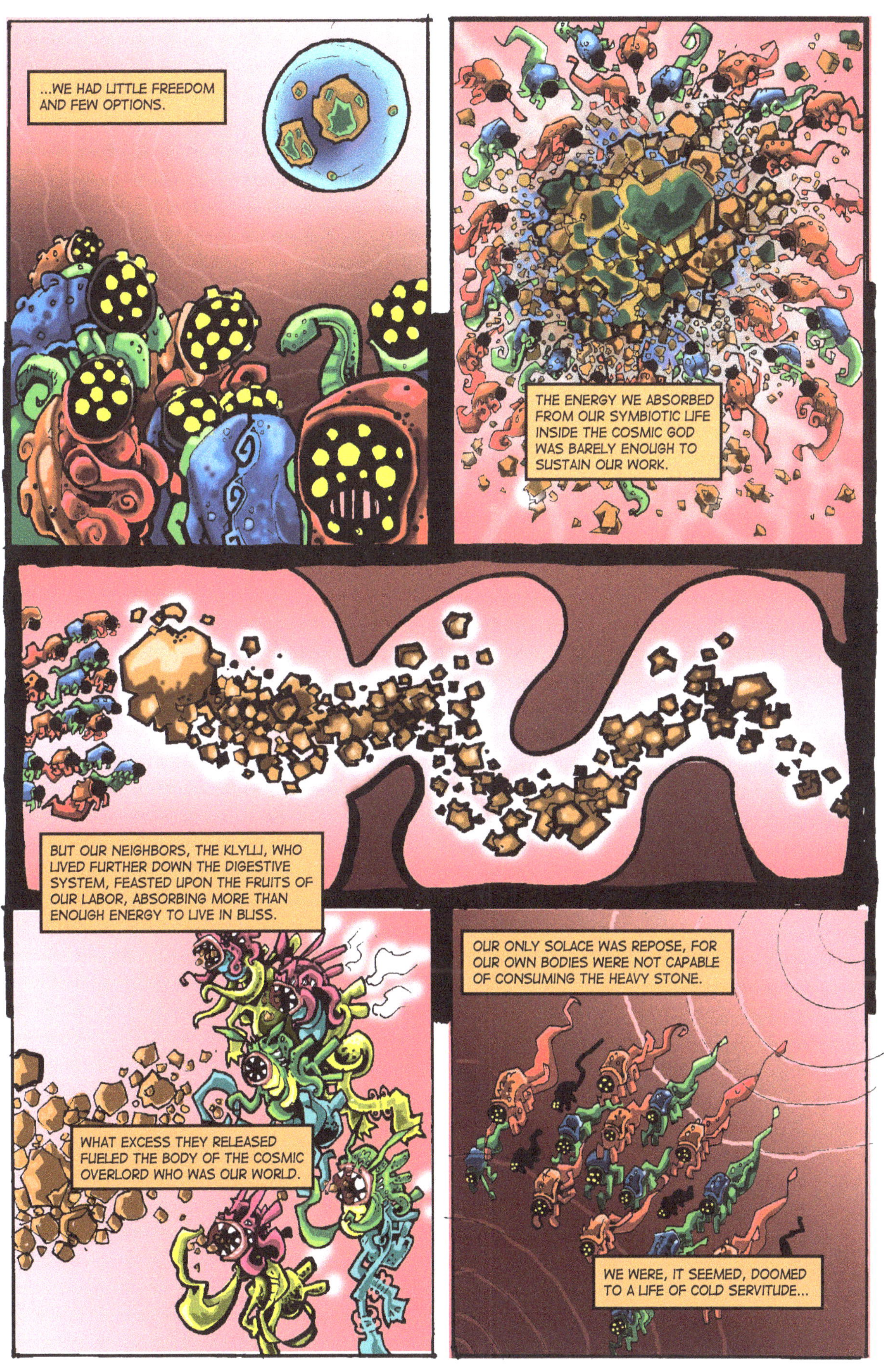

...WE HAD LITTLE FREEDOM AND FEW OPTIONS.

THE ENERGY WE ABSORBED FROM OUR SYMBIOTIC LIFE INSIDE THE COSMIC GOD WAS BARELY ENOUGH TO SUSTAIN OUR WORK.

BUT OUR NEIGHBORS, THE KLYLLI, WHO LIVED FURTHER DOWN THE DIGESTIVE SYSTEM, FEASTED UPON THE FRUITS OF OUR LABOR, ABSORBING MORE THAN ENOUGH ENERGY TO LIVE IN BLISS.

WHAT EXCESS THEY RELEASED FUELED THE BODY OF THE COSMIC OVERLORD WHO WAS OUR WORLD.

OUR ONLY SOLACE WAS REPOSE, FOR OUR OWN BODIES WERE NOT CAPABLE OF CONSUMING THE HEAVY STONE.

WE WERE, IT SEEMED, DOOMED TO A LIFE OF COLD SERVITUDE...

...THAT IS UNTIL WE ENTERED THE ORION SPIRAL ARM OF ONE SMALL REMOTE GALAXY IN THE VIRGO SUPERCLUSTER.

WE KNEW THERE WAS SOMETHING DIFFERENT ABOUT THIS PLANET AS SOON AS WE SAW IT.

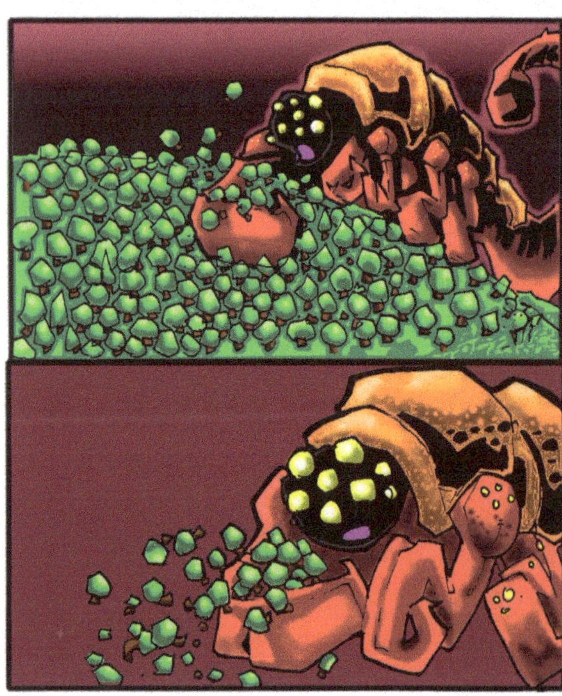

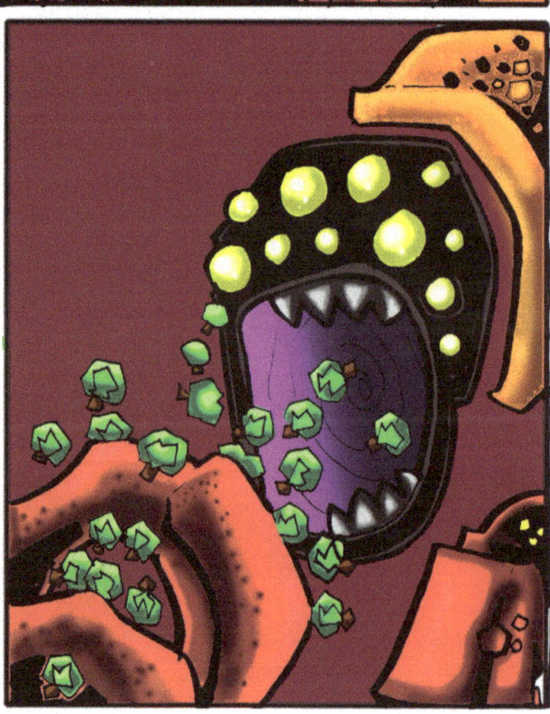

AT LAST, WE HAD FOUND OUR TRUE FOOD.

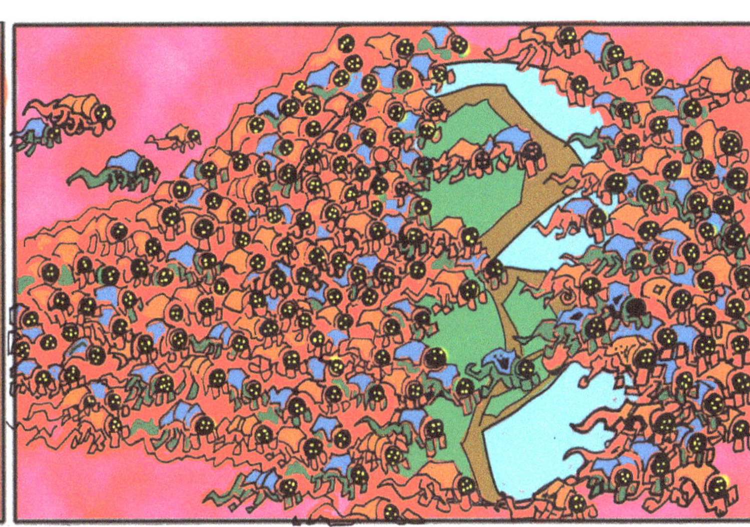

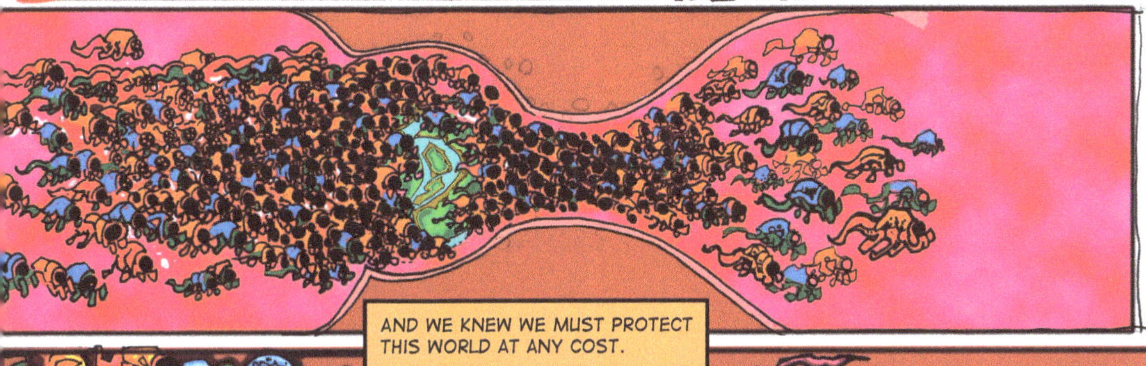
AND WE KNEW WE MUST PROTECT THIS WORLD AT ANY COST.

THE KLYLLI WERE TOO POWERFUL...
ALL WE GAINED FROM RESISTANCE WAS TIME.

BUT TIME WAS ALL WE NEEDED. IT WAS ONLY A MATTER OF WAITING...
...ONLY A MATTER OF HOLDING ON.

OUR PEOPLE WERE NEARLY EXTERMINATED THAT DAY, BUT THEIR SACRIFICE WAS NOT IN VAIN...

...FOR EVERY LIVING CREATURE HAS ITS MEANS OF PRESERVATION... OF RESTORATION...

...OF REPLICATION.

IT WAS A FAR BETTER ENVIRONMENT THAN WE'D EVER KNOWN...
A KIND OF PARADISE.

FOR THE FIRST TIME WE WERE AT THE TOP OF THE FOOD CHAIN.

BUT IT IS THE DESTINY OF EVERY GUT IN THE GALAXY TO BECOME A CAULDRON FOR THE MICROCOSMS, AND TO NURTURE NEW LIFE...

...AND WHO HAS EYES TO SEE WHAT REBELLIONS OR ALLIANCES MIGHT ALREADY BE BREWING...

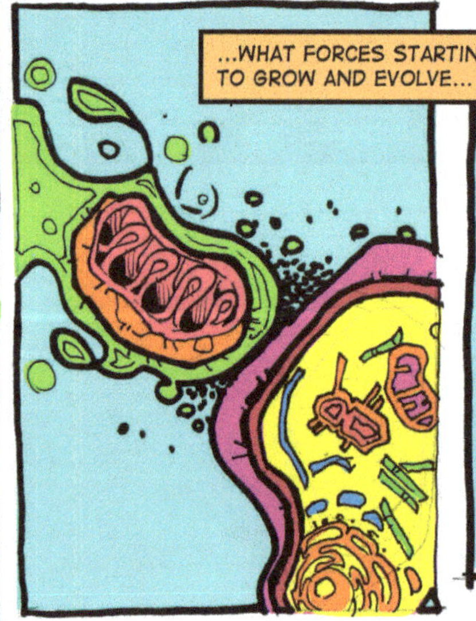
...WHAT FORCES STARTING TO GROW AND EVOLVE...

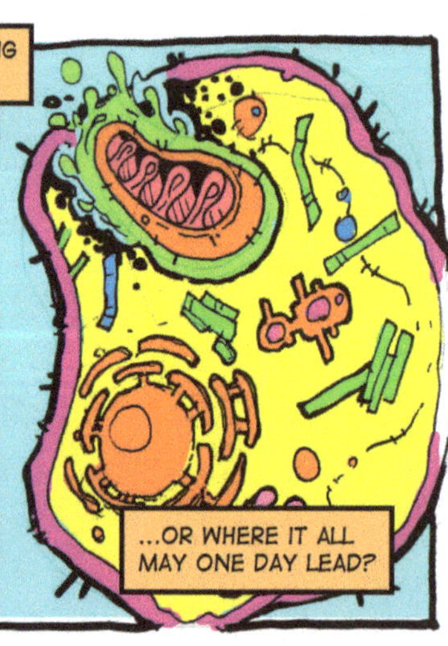
...OR WHERE IT ALL MAY ONE DAY LEAD?

Esmerelda's Tree
by Angela Fullard
Legend has it that the tree in my backyard is cursed...
Walk faster! It's that weird girl...
And since I live here... I'm cursed too.

After school everyone goes over to my neighbor's treehouse...
But I'm never invited.
If I climb to the top and prove that my tree isn't cursed maybe they'll like me.

It shouldn't be that difficult.
I've never been afraid of heights...
Hello?!
or anything for that matter...

I'm not even afraid of spiders.
Hello?
Is there anybody in here?

Besides, I think spiders are more afraid of us than we are afraid of them.
Hello. Are you... losssst?

I guess everyone is afraid of something.
Get back!!!

I'm really sorry!!!
Hissssss
Even me...

When I was little I used to think shadows were monsters trying to capture me.
It's too high...

No matter how fast or far I ran they always caught up to me.
Umm...
SQUAWK!

I was so scared that I would hide under my covers for hours just so that they couldn't get to me.

Ow! Cut it out you fiends!

Until one day...

I figured out that I controlled the shadows. The things that I feared the most for so long were just the ideas in my own head.

Take me to the top!

I was brave...
I could conquer anything.

Maybe it's not that
the kids on my street don't like me.
Almost there!!!
Squeep!

Maybe they didn't even believe in the curse...
Maybe they're just afraid of things they're not used to.

I know now that my tree isn't cursed. Neither am I... we're just different. It might take a long time before the others give us a chance.
What business have you waking me, human child?!
Well...
I was wondering if you would help me build a treehouse?

But if they ever learn to conquer their own monsters...
my treehouse has an open invitation.